MYSTERIOUSLY YOURS, MAGGIE MARMELSTEIN

MYSTERIOUSLY YOURS, MAGGIE MARMELSTEIN

MARJORIE WEINMAN SHARMAT
Pictures by Ben Shecter

1   8   1   7

HARPER & ROW, PUBLISHERS
Cambridge, Philadelphia, San Francisco, London, Mexico City, São Paulo, Sydney
NEW YORK

Mysteriously Yours, Maggie Marmelstein

First Edition

Library of Congress Cataloging in Publication Data
Sharmat, Marjorie Weinman.
    Mysteriously yours, Maggie Marmelstein.

    Summary: Named the mystery column writer for the
school newspaper, Maggie revels in the power she can
exert.
    [1. Journalism—Fiction. 2. School stories]
I. Shecter, Ben, ill. II. Title.
PZ7.S5299My 1982   [Fic]   81-48656
ISBN 0-06-025516-1   AACR2
ISBN 0-06-025517-X (lib. bdg.)

for my mother,
Anna Richardson Weinman,
and all our kitchen talks

• •
****

Contents

• •
****

1
Mystery Person Wanted

● ●
* *

Maggie Marmelstein stared at the notice on the bulletin board at school.

> **Mystery Person wanted.**
> **Apply at Noah Moore's house**
> **after school today.**

"*Mystery person?* Why would Noah want a mystery person?" Maggie asked herself. "And who would apply? Do you get a title? *Maggie Marmelstein, Mystery Person.* That sounds famous and unknown at the same time."

"Do you get paid money for it?" Thad Smith was standing behind Maggie, reading the sign. "I could use some money to buy a new gerbil."

"I have a spare gerbil, Thad." Tamara Axelrod was standing behind Thad. "And I'll be glad to give her to you. Her name is Geraldine because the two g's in a row, as in Geraldine Gerbil, sound ever so nice. But *you* can name her anything you want, Thad."

Tamara smiled at Thad and pretended that Maggie wasn't there.

"Let's hear it for Geraldine Gerbil who sounds ever

so nice," said Ronald the Rock Thrower, who suddenly appeared behind Tamara.

"It's getting ever so crowded around here," said Tamara. "All these little lines forming just to read a sign."

Maggie looked around. Little lines *were* forming in front of the sign. Maggie was glad. It made Tamara seem less noticeable. Tamara was the phoniest person in school. And she was always after Thad.

Maggie saw her best friend Ellen Rudy at the end of one line. Ellen always seemed to be at the end of lines.

"Oh, Maggie," said Ellen. "I don't know what's at the head of this line, but about three out of five lines are worth standing in, so I decided to take a chance on this one."

"This is a definitely worthwhile line, Ellen." It was Noah.

"Noah!" said Maggie. "What does this notice on the bulletin board mean?"

Everyone turned toward Noah.

"Why do you want a mystery person?" asked Maggie.

"I'll explain it after school," said Noah. "But meanwhile Miss Stemmish will give some background information in English class today."

"Background information?" said Maggie. "Is that like a big hint?"

"Does that mean I can get out of this line," asked Ellen, "and just listen to the big hint?"

"If you go to English class now and come to my house after school, you'll know everything you have to know," said Noah.

Maggie, Ellen, and Noah started out for English class. Maggie looked to see if Thad was coming. But he was still listening to Tamara. "Gladys Gerbil is also a perfectly wonderful name and you could still keep the two g's," Tamara was saying.

In the classroom, Miss Stemmish, the English teacher, kept clearing her throat until everyone was seated. Miss Stemmish liked to prepare for her classes by clearing her throat, examining her nails, and if she was in a good mood, humming a soft tune. Today she was doing a little of each.

Miss Stemmish spoke. "As you know, I am the adviser for the school newspaper. And Noah Moore is the editor. So far this year we have published six issues. And now Noah has come to me with a splendid idea for future issues. A Mystery Person column, written of course, by an unknown Mystery Person. Noah, would you please tell us more about it."

Noah stood up. "Presently our newspaper contains columns about sports, music, current events, school happenings, and an editorial. And soon it will feature the Mystery Person column. I'm sure you know that the writers for the columns change from issue to issue so that more of you can get a chance to participate. But the Mystery Person column will be written by one person only."

"I'll write it if you beg me," yelled Ronald the Rock Thrower. "Grovel a little, say pretty please, and salute me every hour on the hour."

"Oh, pretty please, Ronald," said Cynthia Stauffeur. "We're all begging you."

"Right," said Mitchell Fritz. "Begging you to disappear."

"To go on," said Noah. "The Mystery Person can be anyone in school. No one will know his or her identity but me. And whatever the Mystery Person wants to write about will be totally up to the Mystery Person as long as it's not obscene, bordering on the obscene but not quite getting there, defamatory, or libelous."

"Yes, those qualities are definitely out," said Miss Stemmish. "What would the principal think!"

Miss Stemmish and Noah had worked out a format for the newspaper. It was one page, printed on both sides. The principal had insisted upon a small paper. "A front page and a back page and that's it. A nononsense paper. Tiny and trim, just like our school budget."

Both Noah and Miss Stemmish had wanted a larger paper. "Think economy, think ecology, Miss Stemmish," the principal had told her when she asked for "at least four pages, although six would inspire the students to positively leap with creativity."

"They can leap free in the gym, Miss Stemmish," the principal had answered.

Maggie raised her hand. "Tell us about your message on the bulletin board, Noah. Some of us didn't get a chance to read it."

Ellen smiled at Maggie.

"For those of you who didn't have a chance to read my message," said Noah, "it stated that I am having a meeting at my house after school for anyone wishing to apply for Mystery Person. Thank you."

Thad Smith raised his hand. "I have a question in advance," he said.

Miss Stemmish looked at Noah. "Are we answering advance questions?" she asked.

"If we don't have too many," said Noah. He looked around. "Will there be any other advance questions?"

"I have two thousand and sixty-five," said Ronald the Rock Thrower.

"You may ask one of them. Right after Thad," said Noah. "Thad?"

"Um, my advance question is does the Mystery Person job pay money?"

"Hey, that was my four hundred and seventh question," said Ronald.

"There will be no monetary compensation," said Noah. "And now that I've answered both advance questions, I turn the class back to Miss Stemmish with the hope that I'll see all of you at my house this afternoon."

"Isn't this exciting!" said Miss Stemmish. "If I weren't your teacher, I'd try out."

"And I would be happy to have you try out," said Noah.

Miss Stemmish seemed about to hum.

Maggie was thinking, "I'm so mysterious that nobody knows what I'm thinking except me. So *I'm* going to try out, and I'm going to *be* the Mystery Person."

Maggie thought about the Mystery Person all through the day and on her way home from school. When she got to her apartment, she said to her mother, "I'm going to be two people."

"Which two?" asked Mrs. Marmelstein as she stopped beating a cookie batter and looked at Maggie.

"Well, me, of course, and a mystery person," said Maggie.

"A mystery person. Oh my," said Mrs. Marmelstein. "Are you going to hide behind big glasses and an upturned collar and locked doors?"

"I'm not sure," said Maggie. "Noah put up a notice at school that anyone who wants to apply for Mystery Person should go to his house after school. And now I'm on my way."

"I never knew that mysterious people have to try out for it," said Mrs. Marmelstein. "I can't keep up with all these new developments."

Maggie gulped down some milk. "I'm off," she said. "I'll be home for supper."

Mrs. Marmelstein went back to her cookie batter.

"What's going to happen to all the old-fashioned mystery people who just got that way naturally?" she asked.

But Maggie was already out the door and walking down the hall. She stopped in front of the door to Thad Smith's apartment. She raised her hand to knock. Then she stopped. She raised her hand again. And stopped. She started to walk away. Then she stopped, went back, and knocked.

The door opened and Thad peered out. "Maggie! Did you knock?"

"Yes, I did," said Maggie. "Actually it was a noble knock you heard."

"A noble knock? What's that?" asked Thad.

"It's just one of those knocks that's too noble to talk about," said Maggie. "Because I didn't have to knock at all."

"So why did you knock?" asked Thad. "What was the noble knock for?"

"Maybe I'm giving away gerbils," said Maggie, and she started to walk down the hall.

Thad called after her. "Is this your weird day, with noble knocks and stuff?"

"I don't *have* weird days," said Maggie. "I'll tell you why I knocked. I'm going to Noah's house to apply for Mystery Person. I wanted to know if you wanted to go, too. That's what's noble about what I did. I didn't have to do it."

"You don't want me to go, do you?" said Thad.

"I didn't say that," said Maggie.

"Good, because I'm going," said Thad. "You talked me into it."

"Just pretend I didn't knock on your door, gerbil person," said Maggie. "Pretend I'm walking down the hall without you. In fact I *am* walking down the hall without you. 'Bye."

Maggie walked away.

Thad ran after her. "Suddenly I feel very mysterious," he said. "I *want* to try out for the Mystery Person."

"Okay," said Maggie. "After all, the more kids who try, the more exciting it will be for me when *I'm* chosen."

Maggie and Thad walked to Noah's house. It was crowded. Maggie counted twenty-one kids sitting in rows on the floor. Ellen was in the back row. She was sitting beside Thad's best friend, Henry Emery. Tamara was sitting in front of Henry. "Tamara! Why is she trying out for Mystery Person? She's already Phony Person," Maggie thought.

Ellen rushed up to Maggie. Ellen was so shy that she looked embarrassed even while she was rushing. Her face seemed distressed at what her feet were doing. "Oh, Maggie, I don't know what I'm doing here," she said. "I don't want to be the Mystery Person. I have enough trouble just being Ellen. But Noah said I should try, and that could start a habit of my trying all kinds of things."

"That's one of Noah's brightest ideas," said Maggie.

"Thank you, Maggie, and welcome to you and Thad," said Noah, who had been making his way toward them. "We're about to begin."

Maggie and Thad sat down at the end of a row. Noah raised his arms. "Do all of you feel mysterious? Does this meeting have an aura of mystery?"

Ronald the Rock Thrower, who was sprawled out between two rows, piped up. "What's an aura? Is that a horror that lost its h?"

"Quiet, Ronald!" said Maggie.

"Quiet is a riot that went soft!" shouted Ronald.

Ellen giggled. "That's a tiny bit funny, Ronald," she said in a soft voice. "But only a tiny bit."

Maggie knew that Ellen was trying to help. And she did help. Ronald quieted down.

"Most of you already know I am starting a new column in the school newspaper," Noah continued. "And you know it will be written by an unknown person, a Mystery Person. But *who* will that Mystery Person be?"

Tamara stood up. "Here we go," thought Maggie.

"I have a thought I absolutely must share with all of you," said Tamara. "My uncle was a newspaper columnist before he became a dentist."

Tamara stood there, waiting to be admired.

"Shut up, Tamara," said Ronald. "If I have to shut up, you have to shut up."

For the first time since she had known Ronald the Rock Thrower, Maggie wanted to hug him. Tamara sat down.

Noah went on. "I have made a survey and found that our school newspaper is thoroughly read by only forty-one percent of the students, partially read by twenty-seven percent of the students, and totally ignored by the remaining thirty-two percent. Therefore I have concluded that our newspaper needs a shot of adrenaline."

Tamara spoke up. "My grandmother was a doctor. She knew how to give shots."

"I wish she gave you a shot of silence," said Ronald.

Noah continued. "Clearly our newspaper should have something new and intriguing to attract all students. An element of mystery. But the Mystery Person must have two qualities. He or she must be a good writer and be a good keeper of secrets. No one must know his or her identity. So anyone here who hopes to become the Mystery Person and then brag about it had better forget the whole idea."

Everyone looked at Tamara.

"What a perfectly boring idea," said Tamara.

"*You're* a perfectly boring idea," said Ronald.

"To continue," said Noah, "any of you who are interested in competing should write something of approximately one hundred words and give it to me within the next two weeks. It can be fiction, nonfiction, a story, a poem, a sample column, anything."

"How about a grocery list?" said Ronald. "Tomatoes, potatoes, hot dogs . . ."

"String beans!" yelled Mitchell Fritz.

"I wouldn't want to write about string beans," said Dipsey Ford, "because they look so stringy and sad."

"I think I'm getting hungry," said Jody Klinger, who was always hungry.

"Please do not reveal any of your mystery ideas," said Noah. "No matter how strange they are. Now, be sure to include your name, address, and telephone number on your entry. I'm going to put another notice on the bulletin board because I want as many kids as possible to try out. There's even a chance, I'm sorry to say, that the Mystery Person might not be any of you here this afternoon. But you probably have the best chance because you cared enough to come."

Maggie looked at Thad. He really hadn't cared enough to come. He had only come because she had. "You're not going to try, are you?" she whispered to him.

"Are you kidding?" said Thad. "I'm going to write the most exciting, intriguing, mysterious one hundred words I can think of."

2
One Hundred
and Seven Words

. . . .
*********************** ****************

Maggie sat at the desk in her bedroom. Now and then she looked up at the pictures of movie actors that were all over the walls. "Cary," she said to her favorite picture of Cary Grant, "I bet you know something mysterious I could write about. Your head must be full of fantastically mysterious things."

For almost two weeks Maggie had spent her spare time trying to think of the approximately one hundred words that would turn her into the Mystery Person. She wrote poems about windowpanes. She wrote a story about a carrot from outer space. She wrote an essay about Falusha Dagwell, a lady who was never born but should have been, according to Maggie.

Maggie had torn everything up. But the deadline for submitting something to Noah was tomorrow. She had to give him *something*.

"My brain has stopped working," thought Maggie. "Maybe it needs some exercise."

Maggie got up, said "I'm exercising" to her mother, and walked down the hall to Thad Smith's apartment. She knocked on the door. Thad opened it.

"I need exercise," said Maggie, walking inside. "So I walked to your apartment."

"I bet you're exercising your head," said Thad.

"About what?" asked Maggie.

"You know," said Thad.

"You mean the Mystery Person?" said Maggie. "Have *you* thought of anything?"

"It doesn't pay any money," said Thad.

"That's not an answer," said Maggie.

"Is that why you came over here? To find out what I've thought of?" asked Thad. "Well, I'm not *sure* if I'm even trying. But I won't try hard, if I try at all. Just sort of easy."

"That means you haven't thought of anything," said Maggie.

"I didn't say that," said Thad. "Actually I'm waiting for my ideas to come. Like any minute."

"Oh sure," said Maggie.

"I *am*," said Thad. "I'm busy waiting. So maybe you could come back later when I'm not busy waiting."

"I'm busy, too," said Maggie. "With lots of ideas. So I'll see you when *I'm* not busy. 'Bye."

" 'Bye," said Thad.

Maggie walked out of Thad's apartment and down the hall to hers. As she was opening her door, she heard someone come down the hall and stop at Thad's door. Maggie turned around.

Tamara was standing in front of Thad's door. She

was holding a big notebook. "Well, hello, Maggie," said Tamara.

"Well, good-bye, Tamara," said Maggie.

Maggie went into her apartment. "So that's where Thad is getting his ideas! Well, I'll beat him. I'll beat them. I'll beat everybody."

Maggie went to her room. She sat down. "Exercise really helps," she thought. "Maggie Marmelstein is inspired."

Maggie wrote:

```
Dear Boys and Girls,
  I am the Mystery Person. I
sit behind you or in front of
you or beside you or not even
near you in school. I observe.
I pass you in the hallways and
eat with you or don't eat with
you in the cafeteria. I even
say to you, "I wonder who the
Mystery Person is." (A little
tricky, but necessary.) I will
never tell you who I am unless
I get nominated for the Nobel
Prize for Literature. That
would cause me a lot of
identity problems so I
sincerely hope it doesn't
happen. Well, maybe not
sincerely.
            Mysteriously Yours,
            Maggie Marmelstein
```

"Mistake, mistake," muttered Maggie. And she crossed out Maggie Marmelstein and wrote in The Mystery Person. Then she counted the words. "One hundred and seven. Well, that's approximately one hundred."

At the bottom of the sheet Maggie printed her name and address and telephone number. Then she went into the kitchen.

"What do you think of this?" Maggie handed her paper to her mother.

Mrs. Marmelstein sat down and read it slowly and carefully. "You wouldn't want a *Nobel Prize*?" she asked. "Your father and I would go to Sweden with you. You could send back picture postcards to all your friends. Has Cary Grant ever been to Stockholm?"

"I'll ask him the next time I write to him," said Maggie. "But first, do you like this?"

"It has something that I would call flavor," said Mrs. Marmelstein. "Like putting in an extra bit of cinnamon and cloves in fruitcake. It has real flavor, Maggie."

"Then you really like it?" asked Maggie.

"Really flavorful," said Mrs. Marmelstein. "The highest compliment I can give it. That's my top compliment."

Maggie felt happy. She went to her room and reread what she had written. She copied it in her best printing.

Then she thought of another question for her mother. "Do you think like Noah?" she called from her room.

"Maybe here and there, now and then, on occasion and sometimes," Mrs. Marmelstein called back.

"How about always?" Maggie called.

Mrs. Marmelstein came into the room. "Always would make Noah and me twin thinkers," she said.

"You're right," said Maggie. She hugged her mother, carefully packed her paper with her books, and looked forward to the next day. But she couldn't help thinking about Thad and Tamara. "Tamara was standing at Thad's door with her big notebook and her big mouth. Well, I've got a big brain, and that beats everything."

3
"It's Hard
to Stay Mad Forever."

. . . .
* *

At school the next morning Maggie looked for Noah right away. She found him talking to Thad and Tamara.

"Thad and Tamara *again*," thought Maggie. "Thad couldn't like Tamara. Thad *didn't* like Tamara. He didn't but he *does*. At this very awful moment, he does."

Maggie waited until Noah was alone. Then she went over to him. "Here's my entry," she said.

Noah looked down at the paper Maggie had handed him. "I'm so glad you decided to try out, Maggie," he said. "I'm certain you wrote something excellent."

"It has flavor," said Maggie. Then she said, "By the way, I saw Tamara and Thad together. I guess they just happened to be in the same place at the same time, right?"

"That's what I would have concluded," said Noah. "A chance encounter. But I saw them walking down the hall together before they spoke to me. They wanted to make sure that the contest deadline was today."

"So they're *both* entering the contest?" Maggie asked.

"Who *isn't* entering?" said Noah. "I had planned to accept the entries very quietly and privately, so that no one would know who was trying to become the Mystery Person, but there are so many that it doesn't matter if the names of the contestants are known. In addition, some kids who didn't enter will say they did, just for the fun or mystery of it, and some who entered will say they didn't. So with all the information and misinformation, I have every confidence that no one will be able to figure out who the Mystery Person is when I make my selection."

"You're the smartest, Noah," said Maggie. She always liked saying that to Noah, because he was.

"Good of you to say that," said Noah. "But I won't know if my idea was smart or perhaps rather stupid until the Mystery Person is actually writing the newspaper column."

A line was forming in back of Maggie. Everyone was clutching sheets of paper. "They're lining up for you, Noah," she said.

"Yes, we are the Mystery People," said Ralph Nadesky. "Make way for us."

"I am Cynthia the Mysterious," said Cynthia Stauffeur.

"I'm just plain Dipsey," said Dipsey Ford. "But I'm entering anyway."

"Well, don't look so sad about it, Dipsey," said Ronald. "You already look as if you've lost, so what can you lose?"

"I hate crowds," said Jody Klinger. "Crowds make me feel like I'm a part of something much too big."

"You are," said Ronald. "Yourself."

Maggie said good-bye to Noah. "Enjoy your mob," she said to him.

"A mob of mystery, Maggie," said Noah. "Whoever becomes the Mystery Person will have won against a tremendous number of kids."

"Noah's talking about *me*," thought Maggie as she walked away. "Because I'm going to win over everybody. Including Thad Smith and Tamara Axelrod! *Especially* Thad Smith and Tamara Axelrod. I'll show them."

"Maggie! Hey, Maggie." It was Ellen.

"I entered the competition," said Ellen. "But I hope I lose. I'll hope that you win if you hope that I'll lose. I know I'll lose anyway, because I used Ronald's idea about a grocery list."

"I hope what you hope," said Maggie, and they walked to class together.

For the rest of the day Maggie thought about the things that were going to make her happy—like becoming the Mystery Person—and not about Thad and Tamara maybe being friends again.

After school, Maggie saw Thad walking home alone and she caught up with him. "What's new?" she asked.

"New?" said Thad. "As opposed to old?"

"Strange answer," said Maggie.

"Strange question," said Thad.

"No, it isn't," said Maggie. "You just don't want to answer it. Here's another question. Have you forgotten all the tricky things Tamara's done?"

"My memory is perfect," said Thad. "But it's hard to stay mad at somebody forever."

"I think it's easy," said Maggie. "When the somebody is Tamara. Math and Social Studies should be that easy."

"Well, Tamara showed up at my apartment yesterday with what she called super super super contest ideas. She said she had so many super ideas she didn't know what to do with all of her extras. She said I could use them. But I told her I had my own ideas, and I didn't need any of hers. And besides, it's semi-cheating to use somebody else's ideas."

"So far, so good," said Maggie. "Then what?"

"Well then she stuck some papers into my hand. I told her I didn't want them. I said, *'I don't need those ideas.'* Strong, like that."

"Still good," said Maggie. "Go on."

"Well, then she said they were a present and I had to take them. That's what she said. So I took them and read my present. And the ideas were almost super. But I'm not using them. I used my very own mystery idea. It came to me at midnight last night. A very mysterious time."

"But you're friends with her again," said Maggie.

"I said I wasn't mad at her," said Thad. "Did I

say friends? I didn't say friends. Is your mind on vacation today?"

"Maybe it went to Toledo," said Maggie.

When Maggie got home, she went to her room. She spoke to the pictures on her wall. "Bad news, Cary, John, Steve, and all you guys. Thad Smith, whom I have told you about many times, has a mind that is on permanent vacation. It went to Alaska and is now in a deep freeze. But don't worry about it, because it's his problem and not yours."

Then Maggie sat on her bed and wondered why it seemed to be *her* problem.

4
There Is a Winner!!!

The next day when Maggie got to school, she noticed a crowd around the bulletin board. Everyone was pushing close to read it. She rushed to join the crowd. Noah had put up a notice! Maggie read it silently.

> **There is a winner!!! Of course I can't tell you who it is, but this notice is to thank all of you aspiring Mystery Persons. *All* the entries were interesting, but one in particular had a certain irresistible flavor. The person who wrote it is going to be the Mystery Person. Thank you very much. I sincerely hope you will enjoy the column and think of it as a part of your lives.**
>
> **P.S. Please do not follow me to see whom I talk to today. I know it's an intriguing notion to think I'll lead you to the Mystery Person. But I won't. The Mystery Person already knows, simply by reading this notice, that he or she won. Don't ask me how. That's part of the mystery flavor.**

Maggie stared at the bulletin board. "The winner knows by reading the bulletin board. Hmm." Maggie was talking to herself. Everyone was talking to no one in particular. Maggie read the message again. She stopped at the words *irresistible flavor*. And then at the last line: That's part of the mystery *flavor*. "Flavor again," she thought. "That's it! I told Noah my entry had flavor. Now Noah is telling me that I won!! Me!!"

Maggie wanted to shout, "I won!" But she didn't. This was the beginning of her big secret. She made up her mind that she would keep it no matter what.

"I bet the Mystery Person is Ronald the Rock Thrower," said Thad, who suddenly appeared beside her. "He isn't at all mysterious, so he would be perfect. Nobody would think of him but me."

Maggie didn't know what to say. It was one thing to keep a secret, but another to pretend she didn't know who the Mystery Person was. At last she said, "There certainly isn't anything mysterious about throwing rocks. So Ronald is a clever guess."

"I agree," said Henry, who was with Thad.

Maggie liked Henry. He was totally loyal to Thad. If Thad bumbled, Henry cheerfully bumbled along with him. If Henry had any of his own thoughts about the identity of the Mystery Person, he was keeping them private.

"Ronald the Rock Thrower it is," said Henry. "A super, right-on-the-button guess. If only he could write."

"Right! He can't write," said Thad. "That is, not well enough to write a column."

"*I* can," said a voice behind Maggie. It was Tamara. "Nobody knows who the Mystery Person really is," she said. "It could be me. I might be Tamara Axelrod, Mystery Person."

"Are you hinting that you are?" asked Thad.

"Maybe," said Tamara.

Maggie wanted to scream, "You are *not*! I know because *I* am." But she couldn't say a word. Tamara was clever. She knew she wasn't the Mystery Person and she knew the real one would have to keep quiet about it. So Tamara was free to brag.

Thad was staring at Tamara. "Say something mysterious," he said.

"I already did," said Tamara. "I said I might be the Mystery Person."

"That's not mysterious. That's bragging. Right, Thad?" said Henry.

Tamara didn't wait for Thad's answer. She glared at Henry. "I'll be writing my first Mystery Person column soon if I'm the Mystery Person," she said, and she walked off.

"That makes sense, doesn't it Thad," said Henry.

Thad didn't answer. "Hey, Mystery Person maybe," he called, and he ran off after Tamara. Henry ran after Thad.

Maggie just stood there thinking, "Thad Smith is

so impressed by the Mystery Person that he's gone after the wrong one. Well, *I'm* it, even though I can't tell him or anybody. Maggie Marmelstein's got the mystery!"

Maggie went to class. The classroom was buzzing with Mystery Person talk. "All about me," thought Maggie. It was hard to concentrate on schoolwork. She saw Noah a few times during the day, but he merely said hi and walked on.

When school was over, Maggie ran home. Her mother was sewing a curtain in the kitchen. "How are things in the world of mystery?" she asked.

Suddenly Maggie realized that she couldn't tell her mother that she had won. She had to keep the secret from everyone.

"Somebody won," said Maggie.

The telephone rang.

"The door opens, the telephone rings," said Mrs. Marmelstein. "One minute it's just stitch, stitch, and the next all excitement."

Maggie answered the telephone. "It's Noah," said the voice on the line.

Maggie looked at her mother.

"Your face says private," said Mrs. Marmelstein. She picked up her sewing and left the room.

"Hi," Maggie said into the telephone. "I can talk."

Noah said, "I timed how long it would take you to get home if you ran and I knew you would run, that walking wouldn't adequately express your feelings of winning. So hello, full of flavor. Congratulations."

"I won!" said Maggie. "It's really true!"

"Shh," said Noah. "Remember that 'Shh' has to become a habit."

"I'll remember," said Maggie. "It's just that I'm so excited. I filled my wastebasket with ideas before I wrote the winner."

"It had such a sense of intrigue," said Noah. "It was just what I was looking for."

"My mother would be so happy if I could tell her," said Maggie. "But of course I won't."

"You won't have to tell her," said Noah. "I'm sure she'll know."

"*How?* This is supposed to be *our* secret," said Maggie.

"Well, your mother is very observant, and a keen picker-upper of signals," said Noah, "especially from you, her daughter. She can tell by your voice, your walk, what you talk about, what you don't talk about, by any number of things, that you won. So it's best to tell her that you know that she knows, and then you won't have anything to hide. She'll keep your secret, and in addition, she can give her opinion on whether your columns are sufficiently flavorful. Think of her as an invaluable consultant as well as your mother."

"Invaluable consultant. I'll remember," said Maggie.

"I would like to meet with you to discuss your columns," said Noah, "but I think it best that we limit our talks to telephone conversations as much as possible. I'm sure everyone is watching me closely to see whom I talk to. In fact, I think I'm already being followed."

"That makes me feel even more excited," said Maggie. "Like I'm a goal or a prize or something. Follow Noah and find . . . me!! They're looking for me and they don't know it."

"I'm glad you're so excited about this," said Noah, "but we must be *extremely* careful. And don't forget the purpose of all this mystery. Your new column. Do you have any ideas for your first column?"

"My first column?"

"Yes," said Noah. "Did I say something wrong? Are you still there on the other end of the line?"

"I'm right here," said Maggie. "When do you need the first column?"

"Your deadline is next Thursday," said Noah.

"So soon?" said Maggie.

"That's almost a week away," said Noah. "You'll have a week's worth of ideas to work with."

"Right now I don't have a minute's worth," said Maggie. "I'd better hang up and start thinking."

"I have every confidence in you," said Noah. "Good-bye, Mystery Person."

"Good-bye," said Maggie. She hung up.

Every confidence, Noah had said. "That's much too much confidence," thought Maggie. "I don't even have one idea. Well, maybe Thursday will never come. Then again, it will be the first Thursday in recorded history that didn't show up, so I'd better not count on it."

5
"Easy and Fantastic"

• • • • • • • ◦ •
* *

Thad and Henry were walking home from school.

"Tamara is the Mystery Person," said Thad.

"How do you know that?" asked Henry.

"Because she had so many ideas for the contest that she could have been chosen Mystery Person thirty-five times and still have had enough ideas left over for thirty-five more Mystery Persons."

"Maybe her ideas were rotten," said Henry. "Maybe she could have been chosen Rotten Mystery Person seventy times. That's thirty-five plus thirty-five, you know."

"Oh, Thad! Wait, wait!"

Henry turned around. "Seventy Rotten Mystery Persons is in back of us. She wants you to wait for all of her."

Thad turned around. "Do you think she wants to tell me her idea for her first column?"

"Pretend, if you wish," said Henry. "And you *are* pretending. If Tamara is the Mystery Person, I'm the Invisible Man."

"I can't see you," said Thad.

"Then you won't know I'm gone," said Henry. "Good-bye, Thad. I'm leaving you with Tamara. Lots of luck."

"Stay!" said Thad. "I can see you. Your shirt is red, your hair is brown, your eyes are . . ."

But Henry walked off.

Tamara caught up with Thad.

"I know you want to talk to me," she said. "You ran after me today. You think I'm the Mystery Person."

"I did, but I don't," said Thad. "For one little running minute and for part of the way walking home, I did. But Henry doesn't think you're the Mystery Person and Henry knows these things sometimes."

"You want to know who the Mystery Person is, don't you?" said Tamara.

"I do?" asked Thad. "Why?"

"Because whoever discovers who the Mystery Person is, is more important than the Mystery Person."

"How come?" asked Thad. "I mean, how does that work? The Mystery Person is the Mystery Person. The person who discovers the identity of the Mystery Person is still not the Mystery Person. It's okay to be a discoverer, but it's not that special."

"What if you discover and then *tell*," said Tamara. "Think about it. Think of the glorious, glorious, glorious moment when you *tell*. We could discover and tell together."

"I don't want to do anything together with you," said Thad. "You play tricks. I remember your tricks

from the campaign for class president."

"So you don't want to do something easy and fantastic?"

"What's easy and fantastic?" asked Thad. "I don't want to do it, but what is it?"

"Watch Noah, that's what it is. Watch everything he does, whom he talks to, whom he avoids. The last is very important. It could be the Mystery Person. Do you think I'm smart, Thad?"

"Um."

"Say it."

"Um."

"That's good enough. I know exactly what you mean. And thank you."

"Um, sure."

"So don't forget the plan. And we'll talk to each other each and every day to see what we've each found out."

"We will?"

"Good. Then we're in this together. And it's going to be fantastic, fantastic, fantastic."

"It is?"

6
The First Column

. . . .
****

"I know that you know," Maggie said to her mother.

"Oh good, Mystery Person," said Mrs. Marmelstein. "That means I can congratulate you out loud instead of to myself. I knew the minute you walked in the door. Your feet touched the ground too briefly."

"Noah knew that you knew but I didn't know you knew, so maybe you and Noah are twin thinkers after all," said Maggie. "He wants you to be my invaluable consultant for the column."

"I've never had a title like that," said Mrs. Marmelstein. "And *I* can't tell anyone either."

"Yes, 'Shh' has to become a habit," said Maggie.

"Shh. I'll remember that," said Mrs. Marmelstein.

Maggie went to her room. "Tomorrow is Saturday. No school. But I will get up early, I will sit down at my desk and immediately write the entire column. I just know it will happen that way." Maggie looked up at her picture of John Wayne. "I have nothing to worry about, John."

On Saturday Maggie got up early. Her mind was blank. "This is a Saturday-morning disaster," she thought. Then she smelled something good coming from the kitchen. "Empty stomachs lead to blank minds." Maggie went into the kitchen.

"I'm baking Mystery Muffins," said Mrs. Marmelstein.

"What's in them?" asked Maggie.

"That's my mystery," said Mrs. Marmelstein. "But you may eat as many as you want."

Maggie tasted a muffin. "You put cinnamon and cloves in these, didn't you?"

"Among other things," said Mrs. Marmelstein. "Remember what I said about real flavor? Now what kind of real flavor are you putting in your first column?"

"I'm stuck," said Maggie. She smiled. "Maybe I'll write about cloves and cinnamon."

"As your invaluable consultant, I think you should skip cloves and cinnamon in your column," said Mrs. Marmelstein. "They're exciting in muffins and boring in columns."

"So what's exciting besides cloves and cinnamon?" asked Maggie. She took another bite. "Wait! Movie stars are exciting."

"Like Cary Grant?" said Mrs. Marmelstein.

"Right," said Maggie. "And I could tell the kids everything I know about him. I even know what toothpaste he uses."

"Cary Grant's toothpaste?" said Mrs. Marmelstein. "In Column Number One?"

"Well, maybe not," said Maggie. "Besides, then everyone would know that Maggie Marmelstein wrote about Cary Grant's toothpaste. Who else would have information like that? I would give away that I'm the Mystery Person."

"Yes, Cary Grant's toothpaste would definitely be a giveaway," said Mrs. Marmelstein.

"Still, it would be fun to write about an exciting person," said Maggie.

"Even without their toothpaste," said Mrs. Marmelstein.

"Well, maybe they don't have to be famous," said Maggie. "Maybe they could be regular people."

Mrs. Marmelstein handed Maggie another muffin. "What kind of regular people?" she asked.

"I only know one kind," said Maggie. "Regular people like me and like you."

"Like you sounds good," said Mrs. Marmelstein.

"Hey, I could write a column about *kids* I know," said Maggie. "Or maybe one kid at a time. A personality profile. I see them in magazines."

"I see them, too," said Mrs. Marmelstein. "They tell you all sorts of things you don't want to know about people you don't want to know."

"This would be different," said Maggie. "It would be about kids you'd like to know better. I could start with someone really super."

"Like super who?" asked Mrs. Marmelstein.

"Like . . ." Maggie was thinking. "Like Ellen. Everybody should know Ellen better because it's hard to know Ellen at all."

"Everyone will know that Ellen isn't the Mystery Person if you write about her," said Mrs. Marmelstein. "In fact, everyone you write about will be eliminated as a possibility. You'll narrow the field."

"No," said Maggie. "Because I'll say that anybody I write about in the column could or could not be the Mystery Person writing about the Mystery Person."

"Now *there's* your cinnamon and cloves," said Mrs. Marmelstein. "*That* gives your column the best flavor of all. The flavor of total confusion. I love it, Maggie!"

"So do I," said Maggie. "Thanks for your help, invaluable consultant." Maggie grabbed another muffin and went to her room.

She sat down at her desk and started to write.

```
    Greetings from the Mystery
Person, whoever I may be. For
my first column I am writing
about someone you should all
know better. In future columns
I will be writing about other
people you should all know
better. Anyone I write about
could or could not be the
Mystery Person writing about
the Mystery Person. (I got
this job because I am both
mysterious and careful enough
```

not to give away my true
identity.)

Now I am writing about Ellen
Rudy. If you don't know Ellen,
just step up and introduce
yourself. She will be glad to
meet you even if it seems that
she isn't. Ellen is smart and
friendly and knows what to say
and what not to say. You could
learn from a person like
Ellen.

Ellen was queen in a class
play and did a great job at
it. She also has hobbies like
stamp collecting, and she is
hoping to learn to swim in the
near future. Ellen can be
found in the sixth grade.
Don't forget to look hard if
at first you don't succeed in
finding her. I would not wait
too long to find Ellen, as
this column will make her more
popular than ever.

I am going to finish up my
first column by asking you to
write to me to tell me what
you think of it. Letters and
cards can be addressed to me,
the Mystery Person, in care of
this newspaper.

Thank you for reading my

first column, and I guess you
have read it if you are
reading this.
Mysteriously Yours,
The Mystery Person

Maggie showed the column to her mother.

Mrs. Marmelstein said, "I like it, you like it, and here's hoping that Ellen will like it."

"Oh, I never thought of that," said Maggie. "Do you think she'll mind?"

"Part of her will mind, I'm sure," said Mrs. Marmelstein. "Ellen is very shy, and a newspaper column, by its very nature, is not. I think it will give her some trouble and some happiness."

"But more happiness than trouble," said Maggie, "because Ellen deserves to be known. And when kids get to know her, they'll be her friends."

Maggie called Noah, "I've done it! The first column. A personality profile on Ellen."

"A truly fine idea," said Noah. "Truly fine."

"My mother likes it, too," said Maggie. "So I'm going to print it up nice and neat. Then I'll take it to your house."

"Now *that* may not be a truly fine idea," said Noah. "It may, in fact, be a truly terrible idea. I'm afraid someone could see you going to my house."

"Really?" said Maggie. "Well, I'll make sure no one is watching me. It's all part of my Mystery Person job. See you soon." And she hung up.

Maggie carefully reprinted her column. Then she waved the paper back and forth in front of her mother. "Here it is," she said. "And here I go, off to Noah's house to deliver my very first Mystery Person column."

"Be careful," said Mrs. Marmelstein. "Remember you're on a mission of mystery."

"I'll remember," said Maggie. "I can't let anyone see me deliver this to Noah."

Maggie opened her apartment door and stepped into the hall. Thad Smith was standing there.

Quickly Maggie put the paper behind her back. "What are *you* doing here?" she asked.

"I live in this apartment house," said Thad.

"But not in the hallway in front of my door," said Maggie.

"I was just going to knock on your door," said Thad. "You know how it is to stand in this hallway and knock on a door. Well, that's what I was almost doing."

"Well, if you want to see me, I'm not home," said Maggie.

"Where are you going?" asked Thad. "And what are you holding behind your back?"

"I'm in trouble," thought Maggie. "Why is Thad standing out here? Does he suspect what I'm doing?" Maggie knew she couldn't go to Noah's house.

"I'm on my way to the incinerator to throw out this piece of paper," said Maggie.

"Why is it behind your back?" asked Thad.

"Is there a special place to hold stuff that's going

into the incinerator?" asked Maggie, and she rushed by Thad to the incinerator closet. She dropped her column down the chute.

"How come you're throwing away one thing at a time?" asked Thad. "In my family we save up stuff, and when we have a load, we drop it down the chute."

"I'm a very neat person. See you, Thad," said Maggie, and she went back into her apartment before he could ask any more questions.

"You *are* a mystery person," said Maggie's mother. "How you got to Noah's and back so soon is a mystery to me."

"I didn't go anywhere," said Maggie. "Except to the incinerator. Thad Smith was in the hall. So I've got to call Noah and tell him I can't take the column to him now."

Maggie called Noah and told him what had happened. "I'll have to print a new copy of my column," she said. "Then maybe I can bring it over at midnight."

"Nicely stealthy, but impractical," said Noah. "I don't think you can bring your columns to my house at any time. Thad Smith may be suspicious. Anyone may be suspicious."

"I could mail it to you," Maggie said.

"We can't take that chance," said Noah. "I've recently completed a study of the U.S. Postal Service. Sometimes the mail is quick. But sometimes a turtle can get from one part of town to another faster than a letter."

"Well, how about this?" said Maggie. "I could have my mother bake a cake, only it's hollow, and my column is inside. I could hand you the cake in the lunchroom where everybody is throwing food and messing around with it anyway. Nobody would notice."

"Tasty, but impractical," said Noah.

"How about something with switched briefcases?" said Maggie. "I always see that on TV."

"But we don't normally carry briefcases," said Noah. "Besides, it would make me feel like a secret agent, a profession I have no real talent for. However, your last two suggestions are inspiring. A little of one and a little of the other, and I think we're onto something."

"What do you mean?" asked Maggie.

And Noah told her his plan.

"That's daring," said Maggie.

"Exactly," said Noah. "Let me know if you can do it."

"You bet," said Maggie, and she hung up.

She ran to her mother. "I have to get the colunn to Noah without anyone knowing it," she said.

"That's a big suspenseful challenge," said Mrs. Marmelstein.

"You can help," said Maggie.

"I can? How?" asked Mrs. Marmelstein.

"First, do you have any liver around the house?" asked Maggie.

7
"I Know You're the Mystery Person."

* *

"I know you're the Mystery Person," Henry said to Thad as they tossed a football in Henry's yard.

"You do?" said Thad. "That's more than I know."

"No it's not," said Henry. "First you said that Ronald the Rock Thrower was the Mystery Person. Then you said it was Tamara. That was a neat way to take the heat off of you."

"Neat? Heat? You're all wet, Henry," said Thad. "Nobody thinks I'm the Mystery Person except you."

"Well, we've been pals for a long time," said Henry. "And I can tell when you're a Mystery Person and when you're not. And you are."

Henry tucked the football under his arm and walked over to Thad. He put his hand on Thad's shoulder. "I'm going to help you write your column, pal," he said.

"But," said Thad.

"No arguments," said Henry. "I'll write the top part or the bottom part or the middle. Anything you want. I can also do editorial commentary, humorous bits and pieces, current events as seen through the eyes of Henry Emery, and a poem now and then. I'm a talent."

"If you're so talented, why aren't *you* the Mystery Person?" asked Thad.

"I'll admit I tried," said Henry. "But I wasn't simple enough. I guess I overwhelmed Noah with my versatility. I wrote a little bit of everything—two lines of this, two lines of that, and I ended with the words to an original song. I guess it was all too much for Noah."

"Well, you're not going to get another chance to write," said Thad, "because *I* don't have a column."

Henry threw the football again. "I respect your secret," he said. "I know that you can't even tell your best friend. But I'm going to find out on my own, and when I present the evidence to you, you'll have to confess who you really are. Then we can write the column together."

Thad tossed the football back. "How are you going to do all of that, Henry?" he asked.

"I'm going to watch you and Noah. You and he are going to make contact, and I'll be there to see it and get my evidence," said Henry. "I can do anything I make up my mind to do. Wasn't I your campaign manager for class president? And didn't you almost win?"

"I lost," said Thad.

"You see? You don't know how to express yourself,"

said Henry. "*Almost winning* is much more positive than *losing*. You need me to give your column that certain positive something."

"Just toss the ball, Henry," said Thad.

8
A Terrific Plan

Maggie reprinted her column. Then she did it again. "Maybe it's a good thing that I couldn't deliver this to Noah right away," she thought. "If I had, I wouldn't have had a chance to improve it. Then again, I'm not sure that two more commas and one exclamation mark really improve anything."

Noah had told Maggie to keep the column until the Thursday deadline in case she wanted to make any changes. "Thursday is your deadline for giving me the column. And Friday is my deadline for giving it to Miss Stemmish," he said. And for almost a week they worked out their plan for Maggie to secretly pass the column to Noah on Thursday.

"What a terrific plan we have," thought Maggie as she hurried toward the school lunchroom on Thursday.

"Maggie!"

Ellen caught up with her.

"Is everything okay, Maggie?" she asked.

"Sure," said Maggie. "Do you think something's wrong?"

"Well, sometimes you run after me and sometimes

I run after you and it always comes out even, but lately you haven't been running after me. You don't call 'Hey, Ellen!' and try to catch up with me, the way you used to. So I hope everything's okay."

Maggie stopped and looked at Ellen. She thought, "I've been so busy writing about Ellen that I forgot to pay attention to the real Ellen."

"I'm sorry," said Maggie. "I got a little busy."

"That's all right," said Ellen. "And you don't have to make up for the times you missed running after me. We'll just say it's even as usual, okay?"

"Okay, best friend," said Maggie. And they walked into the lunchroom.

Maggie and Ellen sat down at a long table. A bunch of kids were already there. Noah was at the far end of the table. Thad was sitting next to him. Henry was sitting on the other side of Thad.

"Hello, everybody!" Tamara rushed up. She sat down next to Henry.

"Welcome, Tamara," said Ronald the Rock Thrower. "Lunch wouldn't be the same without you. It would be better. But you're just in time for my figs-and-pretzel auction. What am I bid for five figs and a pretzel?"

Almost every day there was an auction of lunches. Everybody hoped to exchange the food they had brought for something they liked better from someone else.

"I will give you a Thermos of cranberry juice," said

Mitchell. "It's clearly superior to five figs and a pretzel, but I'm a generous person."

"I will take the bid of the generous person," said Ronald. "The generous person who slurps cranberry juice all over himself and turns cranberry red. I will save you from that fate, Mitchell."

Ronald and Mitchell made their exchange.

Maggie said, "I have a delectable lunch today."

"Then why don't you eat it?" shouted Ronald.

"I want to give someone else a chance to try it," said Maggie.

"Maggie Marmelstein is kindhearted and generous," said Ronald. "Let's hear it for Maggie!"

Someone gave a weak cheer.

Maggie's lunches were actually quite popular because everyone knew her mother always included something home baked.

"Today I have something entirely new," said Maggie. "A turnip sandwich and four liver crackers."

Everyone groaned but Noah.

"Do I hear any offers?" asked Maggie.

"My body and soul for liver crackers," yelled Ronald.

"Your lunch does sound delectable, Maggie," said Noah. "I'll bid for it with my tuna fish on rye, three marshmallows, and a can of fruit punch."

"You're nuts, Noah," said Ronald. "You may be smart, but you're nuts."

Henry said, "If I were you, Noah, I would think

this deal over very carefully." Henry felt good giving advice to a smart boy like Noah.

"I think your lunch is strange, strange, strange, Maggie," said Tamara.

"I think it's sad," said Dipsey. "Turnips and liver are so sad."

"I think it's strangely sad and sadly strange," said Thad.

"Good observation, Thad," said Henry.

Maggie held her lunch bag high. "Do I have any other bids?" she asked.

Maggie knew there wouldn't be any.

"Then Noah it is," she said. "He's the highest bidder."

"What's wrong with my body and soul?" asked Ronald.

Noah got up and walked over to Maggie. They swapped lunch bags. Maggie was tempted to say, "Mine has real flavor." But she didn't.

Maggie opened Noah's bag. But she wasn't thinking about food. She had just given Noah her column, folded like a paper napkin in her lunch bag!

Maggie watched Noah. He opened the bag slowly, withdrew the sandwich and closed the bag. He was cool. Maggie smiled. The switch had been a success. She and Noah and Mrs. Marmelstein had known there would be no bidders for a turnip sandwich and liver crackers. Mrs. Marmelstein had baked five experimental batches of crackers before she had hit upon the right combination of ingredients. "Wonderfully vile," she had pronounced the winning batch. "A mere whiff of these will keep bidders away."

Ronald yelled, "Where are the liver crackers, Noah? I don't want to go through life without ever having seen a liver cracker."

"Me neither," said Mitchell Fritz. "I feel deprived."

Tamara suddenly looked alert. "Is there anyone here brave enough to dig into the depths of Noah's lunch bag and come up with a liver cracker?" Tamara leaned across Henry and stared at Thad. "It would be an *easy* and *fantastic* thing to do."

Thad looked back at Tamara. Then he looked at Noah's lunch bag.

Tamara kept staring at Thad. She looked as if she would never stop.

Thad shrugged. Then quickly he reached over to Noah's lunch bag, opened it, and stuck his hand inside. Maggie froze. Henry stared at Thad. He had been watching him closely to see if he made any contact with Noah. Maybe this was it!

Noah was still cool. He pulled Thad's hand out of the bag. He said, "If any of you want to see a liver cracker, all you have to do is ask. Politely."

"Okay, I'm asking politely," said Thad.

"Pretty please with liver on it," yelled Ronald.

Noah reached into his bag and pulled out a brown cracker. He moved it back and forth for everyone to see. Kids from the other tables in the lunchroom strained their necks to get a good look. Maggie's auction had attracted a lot of attention. Noah took a bite of the liver cracker. "Made by Mrs. Marmelstein and delicious," he said, while he did strange things with his jaws. "Would you like a bite, Thad?"

"No," said Thad. "Seeing is one thing, biting is another."

"You're so clever, Thad," said Tamara.

Maggie felt angry. Thad wasn't clever! Stupid was what he was for doing what Tamara told him to do! Next she'd be telling him to fetch her slippers or jump through a hoop.

"All right," said Noah. "Now let's all eat our lunches in peace."

But Henry was more curious than hungry. Did Thad have anything in his hand when he put it in Noah's lunch bag? Henry couldn't be sure.

9
"Congratulations to Me, Henry Emery."

. . . .
* *

Henry didn't take his eyes off of Noah's lunch bag.

At the end of lunch Noah said, "I'm going to save two of my liver crackers for a snack later. It will give my palate an opportunity to run down and then renew itself."

Everybody nodded in the way they always did when they didn't quite understand what Noah was saying, but they were sure it was something intelligent.

Noah placed his lunch bag carefully between two notebooks. Henry was getting more curious. And bold. "Won't that break your crackers, Noah?" he asked.

"Liver crackers are sturdy," said Noah.

Maggie was watching and listening. She was uneasy that Noah's lunch was getting so much attention. Poor Noah! It was bad enough that he had to eat a turnip sandwich and two liver crackers.

Maggie was glad when it was time to go back to class.

Thad said to Henry, "Time to go."

Henry was munching on a carrot stick. His eyes had a faraway look. He remembered how Thad had rushed to sit beside Noah at the lunch table. Henry and Thad had come into the lunchroom together. Without saying anything, Thad had headed straight for the table where Noah was sitting. He had sat down right beside Noah even though there were other empty seats. "What's the big rush?" Henry had asked. "Are we playing musical chairs? Or are you the victim of a magnetic force sweeping you toward Noah Moore?" Thad had replied, "I'm hungry, and Noah isn't a sandwich grabber."

Henry gave his carrot a last determined bite. It was all adding up! Thad rushing to sit beside Noah, Thad putting his hand in Noah's lunch bag. Henry knew he must not lose sight of Noah or the lunch bag. And he must somehow see what was inside that bag. If Thad was the Mystery Person, there might be a clue in that bag.

The next period was Gym. "Gym," thought Henry. "I'll get my chance in Gym. Kids moving around, no real order. Chaos is what I need to get inside that lunch bag."

In the locker room, Noah put his books on the bench while he opened his locker. Henry was three lockers away. "This is it!" he thought. "I've got to get that lunch bag before Noah puts it in his locker. But what can I do to distract him? I could faint. Boys are fainting more these days. It isn't just for girls anymore."

"Ooooooooooooh!" cried Henry as he grabbed his forehead, and slumped down on the bench next to

Noah's books. Everyone turned and looked at Henry. Noah rushed to him. Noah was always caring. "What's wrong, Henry?" he asked.

"Well, there's a possibility I might faint," said Henry. "I'm not sure about it yet. Maybe a glass of water would prevent it."

Noah stared at Henry. "If it's any consolation," he said, "you don't look faint to me. There are certain characteristics common to fainting, and I really think . . ."

"Water, water," gasped Henry.

"Perhaps your body knows more than my mind," said Noah, and he hurried off to get some water.

Henry quickly brushed against Noah's books, and they fell to the floor. Thad and Mitchell Fritz, who were nearby, turned. They were about to pick up the books.

"Stop!" said Henry. "The least I can do for someone getting me a glass of water is to pick up his books."

"I think you *are* sick," said Thad. But he and Mitchell turned back to their own lockers.

Henry picked up Noah's books and lunch bag. He stuck his hand inside the bag. He felt crumbs. "Noah isn't always right," he thought. "Liver crackers do crumble." Then Henry felt a piece of paper. It was folded up. "Aha! This could be it."

Henry quickly withdrew the piece of paper from the bag while he looked around to see if anyone was watching him. Nobody was. He stuffed the paper in his pocket, and then he started to replace the books and lunch bag in their original order.

Just then Noah came back. "What are you doing, Henry?" he asked.

"I felt so faint that I knocked over your books," said Henry. "But I put everything back even more neatly than you would expect of a person in my condition."

Noah didn't seem suspicious. He handed Henry a cup of water. "All I could find was a paper cup," said Noah.

"That's okay," said Henry. "Anything in an emergency." And he drank the water.

"How are you feeling now?" asked Noah.

"Much better than before," Henry answered truthfully. "But I think I have to go to the bathroom."

Henry walked to the bathroom. It was empty. "I need complete privacy," he said to himself, and he walked into a cubicle. He took the paper out of his pocket and read it.

"I knew it! I knew it! It's the Mystery Person's first column. And this proves that Thad is the Mystery Person because he's the only one to get his hand inside of Noah's lunch bag. Congratulations to me, Henry Emery, ace detective and master fainter."

10
Wiggly W's

Henry heard someone call his name. Thad had just come into the bathroom.

"Well, this isn't the best place for a confrontation," thought Henry, "but it is very convenient."

"Are you alone?" he called to Thad from behind the partition.

"Yeah, why?" asked Thad. "Are you really sick? Noah said I should check up on you."

"Well, I've just checked up on *you*," said Henry, and he opened the cubicle door. He handed the column to Thad. "Quick, let's talk about this before someone else comes in."

"What's this?" asked Thad as he looked at the paper.

"As if you didn't know," said Henry.

"It looks like the Mystery Person's column," said Thad. "But how did *you* get it?"

"Let's skip all of that," said Henry. "I've just proven that you're the Mystery Person, and now I want to write the column with you."

"How could you prove it when I'm not?" said Thad. "I didn't print this. Look at the w's. See how wiggly they are. Those are nervous w's. I don't print nervous w's. Think about my w's. Not wiggly. Not nervous. I am not the Mystery Person."

"Well, why didn't you tell me that in the first place?" asked Henry.

"I *did* tell you," said Thad. "Over and over again. I am *not* the Mystery Person. I am *not* the Mystery Person. I am *not* the Mystery Person."

"But you didn't make me *believe* you," said Henry. "You should have made me believe you. And now we're in trouble. This column belongs in Noah's lunch bag. How are we going to put it back without Noah seeing us?"

"What do you mean *we* and *us*?" asked Thad. "I didn't take the column."

"Just a minor detail," said Henry. "Help me, pal."

"All right. All right," said Thad. "So what do we do?"

"I'll knock down Noah's books again, and I'll put the column back in the bag," said Henry. "While you grab his attention."

"How do I grab his attention?" asked Thad.

"I don't know," said Henry. "You've got a really big problem."

Henry put the column back in his pocket and they went to Gym. Noah was standing and waiting for them. Henry whispered to Thad, "How do you think he looks, Thad? Does he look mad? No, happy, maybe. Possibly in-between? Does he look in-between Thad, or what?

Tell me. Did he find out I took his column? What'll I do? Advice! Advice!"

Noah said, "I've been waiting for you, Henry. I've been thinking that maybe you shouldn't go to Gym today."

"Oh, so that's why you're waiting for me," said Henry. "Well, I'm fine. Your water did the trick."

"Water has numerous restorative powers," said Noah. "Unfortunately, water is terribly underestimated."

"Well, I'll put in a good word for water every chance I get," said Henry.

After Gym, Thad and Henry watched Noah as he took his lunch bag from his locker. He placed it firmly between two notebooks. Then they all walked down a corridor together toward their next class. Suddenly Henry said, "Will these attacks never stop," and he fell toward Noah with just enough strength to knock Noah's books and lunch bag to the floor.

Henry had done his part. Now it was Thad's turn. Henry looked at Thad. Thad looked blank. Henry had never seen such a blank look on anyone. Henry glared at Thad. But Thad was still blank.

Tamara rushed up. "Noah," she said, "I saw Henry fall on you. Do you need first aid? My grandmother taught me ever so many things." Tamara stood in front of Noah, watching him closely.

Henry quickly reached into his pocket, withdrew the folded piece of paper, bent down and stuck it in the lunch bag on the floor. Then he handed the books and lunch bag to Noah. The column was returned. It was all over. Even Thad once again came to life. "Whew!" he said to himself. "I'm leaving before Henry has any new projects for me." Thad walked off.

"I will get you a glass of water," Henry said to Noah. "Water will do wonders for you."

Henry almost ran down the corridor as Noah watched in amazement. "He's up, he's down. He's down, he's up. All so confusing," mumbled Noah.

11
Noah's Lunch Bag
Gets Dumped

Henry almost bumped into Maggie Marmelstein.

"What's going on?" asked Maggie. "Did you just fall on Noah?"

"I'm on a water walk," said Henry. "So I really can't answer any questions." Henry walked on.

Maggie could see Noah from a distance. "What's happening?" she wondered. "Why is he with Tamara?"

But Maggie knew she couldn't get involved. She walked quickly by Noah and Tamara. She heard Tamara say "Sit!" to Noah. Maggie kept walking until she was out of sight.

Noah saw Maggie walk by. "Lucky Maggie," he thought. "I imagine that no one has fallen on her recently."

"I said sit!" said Tamara. She walked Noah to a bench and pulled him down beside her. Suddenly Noah remembered his lunch bag. "It fell to the floor," he thought. "Is everything intact?" Noah opened a corner of the lunch bag and looked inside. The column was still there. So were the two liver crackers. And some crumbs.

"What's the matter, Noah?" asked Tamara. "Did your liver crackers break?"

Noah looked at Tamara. Why was she paying so much attention to him? Why was she so curious? He had to get rid of her.

"Everything is fine including my liver crackers," he said. "I just checked."

"Then may I have a liver cracker?" asked Tamara.

"You wouldn't like it," said Noah.

"Please," said Tamara. "I'm an adventurous eater." She held out her hand.

Noah opened his lunch bag just wide enough to take out one cracker. He gave the cracker to Tamara.

"Aren't you having one?" asked Tamara. "I hate to eat alone."

Noah sighed, opened his lunch bag and took out the last cracker. Now there was no food left in the bag. Noah was anxious to put the bag back between his two notebooks. But did Tamara remember that there had been only two crackers left in the bag? Would she wonder why he was saving a supposedly empty bag when there was a trash container just a few feet away?

Tamara made a little face as she ate the liver cracker. Noah tried not to smile. He knew Tamara wouldn't ask for another. Mrs. Marmelstein was so right. The liver crackers *were* wonderfully vile.

"Hey, Noah. You got somebody to finish off your liver crackers. Smart. Smart," Ronald the Rock

Thrower yelled as he walked by.

Tamara, who had been concentrating on chewing the cracker, looked up. "You mean I ate your last liver cracker? Sorry." Then she stood up. "Well, I'm off to my next class. You just sit and rest a bit, Noah. Here. I'll throw away your lunch bag for you. 'Bye."

"No!" said Noah. "I mean you'll be late for class. I'm fine and I can throw away my own lunch bag. The exercise will do me good."

Tamara was looking alert. Noah was wary of Tamara's alert look. She *was* suspicious. He handed her the lunch bag. "Well, if you're going in the direction of the trash can . . ."

Tamara took the bag, walked to the trash can and dropped the bag into it. Noah decided to wait until she was out of sight before he retrieved his bag. As Tamara was about to walk away, Henry came along with a glass of water.

"What did you just do, Tamara?" he asked.

"What do you think I did?" said Tamara. "I threw away an empty bag!" And she walked away.

Henry bent over and tried to pick up the lunch bag while he held on to the glass of water and his books. The water spilled.

Ralph Nadesky yelled, "Let me know if you find anything good in there, Henry."

Tamara turned around and stared at Henry.

Henry bent lower and picked up the lunch bag. He tried to brush away various things that were sticking to it from the trash can. Then he took the bag back to Noah. "This looks like your lunch bag," he said to Noah.

"It used to look like my lunch bag," said Noah.

"Rescuing lunch bags is a new hobby of mine," said Henry. "Lunch bags can be reused and reused. Tomorrow this very bag might hold peanut butter and jelly on pumpernickel."

Noah took the bag from Henry. It was a mess.

It seemed to Noah that everyone was watching him take the bag. Especially Tamara. He said in a loud voice, "Thank you for your apt ecological action, Henry. Reusing lunch bags is an act of good citizenship."

Then Noah moved away slightly. He didn't want to be fainted on for the second time in one day.

12
"Are You Thinking
What I'm Thinking?"

. . . .
****

"It was worth eating those liver crackers for," said Noah over the telephone.

"Then you *like* my first column?" Maggie almost shouted into the receiver.

"Very, very much," said Noah. "It has style. It has flavor. It has a point of view. I hope you can keep up this high standard you've set for yourself. Your next column is due next Thursday, you know. That gives you exactly one week to write it."

"I know," said Maggie. "But I'm not going to start it yet. I'm going to wait until the first column is published and see what the kids say about it. That might give me an idea for my second column."

"But it won't give you much time to write it," said Noah. "The first column won't be published until Tuesday, and the second column will be due just two days later."

"That's plenty of time for a professional writer like me," said Maggie.

"I see," said Noah. "At least I think I see. I had such a strange day that I'm not quite certain what

I'm seeing. First there was Thad sticking his hand in the lunch bag. Then later on the bag temporarily landed in the trash can. Also, Henry fainted on me, and Tamara paid much too much attention to me."

"Lunch bag? Trash can?" said Maggie. "Are we in trouble?"

"No," said Noah. "Just don't stand next to Henry."

Maggie said good-bye to Noah. She went into the kitchen where her mother was cutting a coconut cake into squares. "My liver crackers were a nonsuccess, I hope," said Mrs. Marmelstein. "You rushed through here so fast when you got home that I wasn't sure."

"Well, I was in a hurry to speak to Noah. He likes my column. And nobody bid on my lunch but Noah, and so Noah and I swapped bags."

"Everything worked out perfectly," said Mrs. Marmelstein. She put a piece of cake on a plate and handed it to Maggie.

"No, not perfectly," said Maggie. "Thad Smith put his hand in the lunch bag after I gave it to Noah."

"Thad Smith's hand? In the lunch bag? Why?" asked Mrs. Marmelstein.

"Tamara sort of dared him to," said Maggie.

Maggie started to think about Thad. "Why am I thinking about him?" she asked herself. "I wonder, if I went over there right this very minute, would I find Tamara Axelrod there? Maybe he's finished with her as a friend. I haven't seen them together in a few hours."

"I'm taking a little walk," Maggie said to her mother.

"Before or after coconut cake?" asked Mrs. Marmelstein.

"Before," said Maggie. And she walked out of her apartment and down the hall.

Henry and Thad sat in Thad's apartment, grumbling.

"Some help you were," said Henry.

"You're mad at *me*?" said Thad. "You're something, Henry."

"Well, I'm the only person except for the Mystery Person and Noah who managed to see the Mystery Person's column before it's even printed. And I was generous enough to share it with you."

"If it weren't for those nervous w's, you'd still think I wrote it," said Thad.

"I've been thinking about those w's," said Henry. "And now I'm wondering who they belong to. I mean, we've got a clue, you and I."

"So what are you going to do about it? Go around and ask everyone to write a w for you?"

"I'm going to be alert, that's all," said Henry.

There was a knock at Thad's door. Thad opened the door. Maggie was there. "Was that another noble knock?" asked Thad.

Maggie looked at Henry. She was surprised to see him.

"Uh, I heard that Henry fainted today, so I'm knocking to ask how he is. That's the only reason I'm here.

This is a sick call." Maggie turned to Henry. "How are you, Henry?"

"I've completely recovered," said Henry.

"Good," said Maggie. "My mother will probably bake something for you in honor of your recovery."

"Just as long as it's not liver crackers," said Henry.

"It won't be," said Maggie, and she left.

"Henry, why are you joking about liver crackers?" said Thad. "Just stay away from the subject. Look at all the trouble you got into because you saw me reach for a liver cracker in Noah's lunch bag."

"It wasn't a joke," said Henry. "I want to make sure Mrs. Marmelstein doesn't present me with a gross present." Suddenly Henry leaped up. "Wait a minute! Wait a minute! I just thought of something. Maggie and Noah swapped *lunch bags* today. Are you thinking what I'm thinking?"

"Maggie . . . the Mystery Person?" asked Thad.

"Sure," said Henry. "Say, do you happen to have any of Maggie's w's around?"

13
"One Copy for You,
One Copy for Me."

. . . .
*********** *************************

Noah walked into Miss Stemmish's room early Friday morning with his newspaper columns. It was Noah's job to collect the columns from the writers, read and edit the columns, and hand them in to Miss Stemmish each Friday morning before school started. Miss Stemmish was supposed to tell Noah what could be printed and what couldn't be printed and why and why not. But it never worked that way. Miss Stemmish had a hard time saying no to anything. When Noah first went to Miss Stemmish with the idea for a Mystery Person column, she agreed to it before Noah had a chance to explain it. But Noah explained it anyway.

Every Friday Miss Stemmish reread the columns, typed up the messy ones, and took them all to the printer in the afternoon. She picked up the printed newspapers the following Monday afternoon. Early every Tuesday morning, Miss Stemmish took the newspapers to school for Noah to distribute.

Now Noah was handing Miss Stemmish the columns for next week's paper, including the first Mystery Person column.

"You're right on time as usual, Noah," said Miss Stemmish.

"Yes, and I'll be here on time to pick up and deliver the printed newspapers early Tuesday morning," said Noah. "I consider prompt delivery a basic part of journalism."

"And I'll type up the columns that look particularly distressed, go home for my tea and scones, then take all the columns to the printer at four o'clock today. At four o'clock Monday afternoon, I'll pick up the printed papers, and have them ready for you in school early Tuesday morning."

Noah and Miss Stemmish exchanged this dialogue every time Noah left off his columns. It was an advertisement of their mutual reliability. Noah was telling Miss Stemmish she could count on him, and Miss Stemmish was telling Noah he could count on her. The principal had once told Miss Stemmish that reliability was a bigger asset than money.

Miss Stemmish always photocopied the columns and gave the originals back to Noah. "One copy for you, one copy for me," they had agreed when they first started the paper. "Just in case one gets lost." They decided not to tell the principal. He was always complaining that the photocopy machine was overused. "Grocery lists, dentist's bills, recipes . . . waste, waste, waste."

"This is a thrilling day," said Miss Stemmish as she returned from photocopying the columns. She handed the originals back to Noah. "I'll be the first person to read the Mystery Person column with the exception of you and the Mystery Person."

"I can't comment on that," said Noah, thinking of Mrs. Marmelstein. "Let's just say you're in the vanguard of readers."

Miss Stemmish was reading the column. "Why, it's about Ellen," she said. "And so beautifully written. By one of my students, I hope. But don't tell me because of course you can't." Miss Stemmish seemed impressed by her own logic.

"Do you really like the column as much as I do?" asked Noah. "I value your opinion, Miss Stemmish. I really do. And it doesn't have to be the same as mine for me to value it."

"What a lovely thing to say," said Miss Stemmish. "Well, as beautifully written as it is, the column does have two commas and an exclamation mark that I'd love to take out, and then it will be all the more graceful to read."

"You're in charge of take-outs," said Noah. "I'm going to class."

Miss Stemmish looked pleased. She murmured something about "in charge." Then she repeated the words, singing them in a soft voice.

Noah walked out of the room. "Two major accomplishments early in the day," he thought. "The first Mystery Person column is on its way into print. And Miss Stemmish is singing."

14
Following Maggie Marmelstein

. . . .
****

"I've never followed another human being before," said Henry. "Once I followed a dog to see if he got home all right."

It was Friday afternoon. Thad and Henry were walking one block behind Maggie Marmelstein.

"Won't she be suspicious if she sees us?" asked Henry.

"No. I see Maggie all the time and she sees me all the time," said Thad. "Sometimes we're far apart, and sometimes she's breathing down my neck. We have all kinds of combinations of seeing each other."

"Well, I hope she meets Noah soon," said Henry. "This isn't my kind of activity. I'm not your basic follower."

"I think she's going into Rossi's Market," said Thad. "She runs errands there for her mother."

"Maybe she's meeting someone inside. Like Noah," said Henry. "Maybe we'll find out right in Rossi's Market that Maggie is the Mystery Person."

"But we can't just follow her in and stand there like a couple of idiots," said Thad. "We have to buy something. Do you have any money?"

"Three cents," said Henry. "I've been carrying them around for a week, waiting for two more cents. You can buy something with a nickel."

"I don't have any money," said Thad. "I spent my allowance on a new gerbil. So let's hope there's something for three cents in Rossi's."

Thad and Henry followed Maggie into Rossi's Market. Maggie was buying a head of cauliflower. When she saw Thad and Henry she said, "What are you doing in here?"

"Buying, of course," said Henry.

"What?" asked Maggie.

"Three cents' worth of merchandise," said Henry. "Say, Mr. Rossi, what do you have for three cents? We're not interested in cauliflower."

"I have small pieces of chocolate wrapped in foil," said Mr. Rossi. "They're usually ten cents each, but for customers who have only three cents, they're three cents."

"I'll be in with the seven cents next week," said Henry, handing Mr. Rossi three cents. Mr. Rossi handed him the chocolate. Henry held it up. "Who would like a bite?" he asked.

"Let's swap bites," said Maggie. "Cauliflower for you two, chocolate for me."

"Come on, Henry," said Thad. "Time to leave."

"Are you sure?" asked Henry.

"Positive," said Thad. "Good-bye, Mr. Rossi. Good-bye, Maggie."

Thad pulled Henry from the store. "But Maggie's still in there," said Henry.

"And Noah isn't in there," said Thad.

"But what if Noah shows up?" asked Henry.

"We can wait at the corner and watch the store," said Thad.

Henry and Thad stood on the corner.

"Hey, there goes Maggie now," said Henry. "She's heading for home. And no Noah in sight. I'm getting tired of this. Would you like a chocolate?"

"No, you eat it," said Thad. "Are you giving up on trying to find out if Maggie is the Mystery Person?"

Henry put the chocolate in his pocket. "No," he said, "but why don't we go with the wiggly w? Let's try to get a sample of Maggie's w and see if she wrote that column. It sure beats following her around, and owing Mr. Rossi seven cents."

"But how do we get a sample?" asked Thad.

"We? *You*," said Henry. "I'm leaving you in charge of the w's. See what you can do."

"Me?" said Thad.

Henry walked off.

Thad walked home. He was in front of his house when he heard, "Thad! Thad!"

Thad turned around, but he already knew who was calling him. "Hello, Tamara."

"So?" said Tamara.

"So what?" asked Thad.

"So I'm reporting in. I think there's something suspicious about Noah and his lunch bag, but I haven't figured it out yet. And you haven't been doing *your* share of our work. You haven't called me, or come up to me at school or anything. Do you have any information about the Mystery Person?"

"Um," said Thad.

"Do you or don't you have any news?" asked Tamara.

"No news," said Thad.

"It isn't fair for me to do all the work," said Tamara. "Did you notice how I'm always checking in with you at school but you're not checking in with me?"

"I noticed," said Thad.

"Well, are you watching Noah?"

"Sure," said Thad.

"Well, try to learn something," said Tamara. "That's what the watching is all about!"

Tamara turned and marched off. Thad watched her. "I could have told her about the column with the wiggly w's," he thought. "I could have told her that Henry and I think that Maggie Marmelstein might be the Mystery Person. But I can't tell on Maggie. Maggie isn't exactly perfect and now she has that horrible noble knock and she's even nasty when she's buying cauliflower, but she's my friend."

Thad walked up the stairs to his apartment house. "My friend Maggie Marmelstein," he said. "Sounds stupid, but it's true."

15
Maggie the Star

Maggie began to wonder why Thad was paying so much attention to her. All weekend he kept asking to look at her homework. But Maggie turned him down. Then on Monday Thad gave her a "I wish you a wonderful week" card. When Maggie thanked him for it, he said, "It would be wonderful to get an 'I wish you a wonderful week' card back. Could you print me one?"

"No!" said Maggie. She wanted to print him a "Dump Tamara" card. If Thad really wanted her to have a wonderful week, that's what he'd do.

"I'll have a wonderful week anyway," Maggie finally decided. The Mystery Person mystery was causing all kinds of excitement and activity, whispers and strange remarks. And on Tuesday the first column would be published!

When Tuesday came, Maggie made sure that she didn't get to school early. "It could make kids suspicious." She decided that she would walk into school at her usual time, stop and talk to a few kids, and then casually pick up a copy of the newspaper. Copies would be piled in every classroom. Maybe she would walk by a pile, and then suddenly pretend to notice it, and go back and pick up a copy.

But when Maggie got to school, Ellen was waiting for her by the door. "Oh, Maggie," she said. "I'm in the newspaper. The Mystery Person wrote about *me*! I haven't even seen it because I'm too scared to look. But three kids came over and teased me about it."

Maggie felt terrible. She had hurt her best friend, and she couldn't even confess.

Ellen went on. "You always have so much to say, Maggie, and now you don't have anything to say. But that's okay because *I* feel like talking."

"You do?" said Maggie.

"More than I ever have in my life, I think," said Ellen. "Wait till I tell you what happened next."

"Next?" said Maggie.

"Yes, a bunch of kids gathered around me, asking questions about me and being especially friendly. I think they think I'm interesting, Maggie. They listened carefully to all my answers. I feel like a movie celebrity." Ellen giggled. "Maybe you'll put my picture on your wall next to Cary Grant. Well, maybe quite a bit underneath him."

"Then you're happy about the column?" asked Maggie.

"Yes, it's the most exciting thing that's ever happened to me," said Ellen. "But I'm still afraid to look at the column. Will you look at it with me, Maggie?"

Maggie forgot all about her plan. She dashed ahead

of Ellen and grabbed a newspaper from a pile. There was her column on the front page! It *did* look important. First Maggie read the words The Mystery Person because they looked the most important of all. Then she read the column. It had been printed without one word changed, although two commas and an exclamation mark had been removed.

Maggie handed the newspaper to Ellen. "Read it. It's fantastic!" she said.

"You're sure it's fantastic?" Ellen asked as she took the newspaper from Maggie. Ellen started to read without waiting for Maggie's answer. Maggie thought that Ellen looked terrified.

"Well?" asked Maggie.

"Is that really me?" Ellen asked. "I sound like someone *I'd* like to know."

"Good," said Maggie. "Great!" Then she said, "By the way, has anyone asked you if *you're* the Mystery Person?"

"Nobody," said Ellen. "And I have no idea who the Mystery Person is. But it must be somebody who knows me and likes me."

Maggie gulped. Ellen had stumbled onto a clue to the identity of the Mystery Person without even trying. Other kids could pick up the clue, too.

"Everybody who knows you likes you," said Maggie, as somebody grabbed Ellen's arm and pulled her away.

"I heard that," said Ronald the Rock Thrower. "You

were talking to me, right? I wish the Mystery Person would write about me. Then everyone would find out all at once how wonderful I am. Now they have to find out slowly, slowly."

"Hey, Ronald, maybe you really *want* to be in the Mystery Person's column," said Mitchell Fritz.

"But there are no words wonderful enough to describe me," said Ronald.

"Ellen is lucky," said Dipsey Ford. "It must be fun to be lucky."

"You're lucky. You know *me*," said Ronald.

"That's why Dipsey always looks so sad," said Mitchell.

"I'm going to talk to Ellen," said Dipsey, "and see how it feels to be lucky. It must do wonders for your glands and your hair and the bottoms of your feet. Do you suppose good luck spreads all over your body?"

Maggie had never felt so important. Even when she was princess in the class play. That was just make-believe. This was real life. She could make Ellen popular. She could probably make somebody unpopular if she wanted to. She had the power to do almost anything she wanted. Maggie saw Tamara reading the newspaper. Maggie knew she couldn't make Tamara unpopular because Tamara had done that all by herself. Except with Thad.

"I am now the star of the school," she thought, "even though Noah and I are the only kids who know it. Look at the teachers over there. They're trying to guess the Mystery Person's identity. And some of the kids are making bets."

Maggie saw Thad at a distance. He was walking and reading the newspaper at the same time.

Tamara rushed up to him and said, "I see that you're reading the Mystery Person column."

"Sure," said Thad. "And the sports column and the music column and all the other columns. I'm a big reader."

"But you read the Mystery Person column first," said Tamara.

"I'm not saying I did, but if I did, how would you know that?" asked Thad.

"Your nose was near it," said Tamara. "If your chin had been near it, then that would mean you were reading something above it. I saw you pick up your newspaper and I saw where your nose and chin went first. See how observant I am?" Tamara gave Thad's newspaper a little tug. "Have a good time reading, reading, reading," she said.

Maggie studied Tamara. Why wasn't she waving the newspaper and saying, "*I* might be the Mystery Person"? What was going on in Tamara's head? And out of her mouth? What had she said to Thad Smith?

"Who cares?" thought Maggie. "I'm a success and someday Thad Smith will know it!"

Maggie and Noah exchanged quick smiles during

the day. When Maggie got home, she rushed to call him.

"Congratulations! You're a real star, Maggie," said Noah. "A very successful column, and everybody is reading the newspaper. Those piles of newspapers used to *sit*, while the world passed them by, so to speak. Today they were actually grabbed, clutched, and even torn. Marks of real success." Noah paused. "And now we have to talk about the future. Specifically lunch bags. We must change the food. The liver crackers have become famous. *Conspicuous.*"

"We have another problem, too," said Maggie. And she told Noah about her conversation with Ellen.

"That's not a problem," said Noah. "I thought it was clever of you to write about your best friend. The Mystery Person wouldn't dare to write about a best friend in the first column, right?"

"You're saying that something stupid was clever?" asked Maggie.

"I'm saying that something clever was clever," said Noah.

"Yes, I guess it was," said Maggie. "And it's changed Ellen's whole life."

"Her whole life?" said Noah.

"Well, practically," said Maggie. "The Mystery Person can do practically anything."

"Anything?" said Noah.

"Noah, just about the whole school wants to be in

the Mystery Person column," said Maggie. "Even Ronald the Rock Thrower. But I haven't decided yet who will be the lucky subject of my next column. But it will be somebody who really needs my help."

"Maggie, this is supposed to be a Mystery Person column, not a first-aid kit."

"Everybody's reading your newspaper, Noah," said Maggie. "Think about that."

"I'm thinking about that," said Noah. "I am also thinking you're changing from Mystery Person to Too Important Person."

"No, I'm not," said Maggie. "I'm just a humble and modest Mystery Person."

"That sounds better," said Noah.

"Who can do practically anything," Maggie added.

16
A Big Shove for Dipsey

"I'm a success," Maggie said to her mother.

"Of course," said Mrs. Marmelstein as she read the newspaper Maggie had just given her. Maggie had taken only one copy from school. "Better for *me* to take some extras," Noah had said. "Everyone will be looking for a hog newspaper grabber alias the Mystery Person."

"And is Ellen enjoying fame?" asked Mrs. Marmelstein.

"Oh yes," said Maggie. "Someone even asked for her autograph. And now I'm going to start my second column. It has to be finished by Thursday, but I'm a fast professional."

Maggie went to her room and sat down at her desk. "Who should I write about? Whose life should I change? I bet I could get the whole school to love Ronald the Rock Thrower. I could go down in history for doing that. But Ronald would never admit that the Mystery Person helped him. He would just joke about it. Ellen was so happy to be in the Mystery Person column. Who else would be happy?"

Suddenly Maggie started writing. "This is so easy that I should have thought of it immediately. I have the perfect subject. Dipsey Ford! Dipsey, Super-Sad Person, who next week at this time will be the new, improved, popular, and totally cheery Dipsey Ford."

Maggie wrote:

This Week's Column is about Dipsey Ford. Dipsey is a good singer and she plays the flute, which most kids can't do, and she's excellent in sports. In her spare time she takes care of her beautiful plants. Dipsey's plant collection is probably the best of anybody's, and I predict she will win a big plant prize someday soon.

But, as you may have noticed, Dipsey looks a little sad. I know that Dipsey, with some help, could look really cheerful. As the Mystery Person for this entire school, I can help her look that way. Here's my help. Instead of looking sad all the time, Dipsey should try to look sad about half the time, and then work her way

down to one fourth and so on.
If you tell funny jokes to
Dipsey, that might help, but
I'm not sure. If you tickle
her, she will have to laugh,
so think about that. See what
you can do for Dipsey Ford.
                    Mysteriously Yours,
                    The Mystery Person

Maggie read her column. Then she took it to her mother. "This one was quick, Maggie," said Mrs. Marmelstein.

"I told you I'm a fast professional," said Maggie. "Well, what do you think of it?"

"First I have to read it," said Mrs. Marmelstein.

Mrs. Marmelstein sat down and read the column. "Well," she said, "the first part is very nice. The plants especially. Liking green growing things tells us something nice about a person. But the second part . . . well, Maggie, maybe Dipsey Ford is happy looking sad."

"I can tell she isn't," said Maggie. "And the Mystery Person can help her just like the Mystery Person helped Ellen."

"But that was just a little nudge," said Mrs. Marmelstein. "This is more like a big shove."

"Dipsey Ford needs a big shove," said Maggie. "Have you ever seen her?"

"Twice. And she looked fine both times. A little

sad, but maybe she was wearing too tight shoes or she had just read a sad book."

"Well, she'll be grinning from ear to ear after she reads this," said Maggie.

The next day Maggie walked to school faster than usual. "I can hardly wait to get to school and hear the kids talk about me when they don't know it's me."

"Maggie!"

Maggie turned around. Ellen was running to catch up with her. "Want to hear about my new life, Maggie? It's new since yesterday. Well, this afternoon I'm going to show five kids how to collect stamps. And Cynthia Stauffeur said it would be great to take swimming lessons together. And two kids are going to call me up but they didn't say why."

Maggie hugged Ellen. "Will you be too popular to be my best friend?"

"Never, Maggie. But I'd like to be friends with the Mystery Person, too. Before the column was printed I was invisible, and now I'm, well, visible. It's like magic or something."

"Magic," Maggie was thinking. "*I* have the magic."

When they reached school, Ellen said, "Look who's talking to who. Is that good English?"

Thad and Tamara were standing and talking in front of the school.

"I don't care," Maggie told herself. "I'm too important to care about boring little things like that."

17
"Weird Is Wonderful."

****
• •

It was Thursday.

"Time for another lunch bag swap," Maggie said to her mother.

"Yes, and my cauliflower cookies should work as beautifully as my liver crackers," said Mrs. Marmelstein. "No one will want your lunch, Maggie. They'll run a mile to escape from cauliflower cookies, I guarantee."

Maggie walked to school. "The lunchroom has become the most exciting place in school," she thought. "At least for Noah and me."

Maggie and Noah had decided to arrive a little late for lunch so that the table they usually sat at might be filled. "I'd rather not have the same audience as last Thursday," said Noah. "But I don't want them to think I'm avoiding them on purpose." They also decided to arrive separately.

Noah went into the lunchroom first. "Hey, Noah!" shouted Henry. "Hurry up. Thad and I saved a place for you and Maggie."

"You didn't have to do that, Henry," said Noah.

"Yes, we did," said Henry.

Thad kicked Henry under the table, and gave him a dirty look.

"Listen, I've got ten cents invested in this now," Henry whispered to Thad. "You're not getting anywhere with your w's, so I've taken over the leadership." Henry called to Maggie, who had just entered the lunchroom. "Hey, Maggie, we've saved a seat for you!"

"Well, shall we all eat," said Tamara, who had arrived at the table first. "I've been sitting here ever so long."

"I would like to auction my lunch," said Maggie. "And I have a delectable one. Today, among other things, I have cauliflower cookies."

"My favorites," said Noah. "My family has been eating them for generations. I bid my lunch for your lunch, Maggie. I have a sardine sandwich on rye and assorted other goodies."

"Sounds wonderful," said Maggie.

"This table isn't normal," said Ronald the Rock Thrower.

"I think those two lunches deserve each other," said Mitchell Fritz.

Henry said, "I don't understand your lunch, Maggie."

Thad kicked Henry under the table.

Tamara looked as if she were about to say something. But instead she stared at Maggie's lunch bag.

Maggie handed her lunch bag to Noah, and Noah handed his lunch bag to Maggie.

Tamara was smiling.

"I don't like that smile," thought Maggie. "Tamara's smiles never mean what other kids' smiles mean."

Tamara asked, "What else did you get besides cauliflower cookies, Noah?"

Noah opened his bag carefully and pulled out a sandwich. "Oh, a nice, hearty peanut butter sandwich."

"That's interesting," said Tamara.

"I would like to auction my dessert," said Henry. "I have here a foil-wrapped piece of chocolate from Rossi's Market. I would prefer to auction it for money."

"I'll give you twelve cents for it," said Mitchell Fritz.

"You mean, twelve cents, just like that?" asked Henry.

"Take it or leave it," said Mitchell.

"I'll take it," said Henry. Now he kicked Thad under the table.

"This is *such* an interesting lunch," said Tamara. "Isn't it, Thad?"

"I thought the chocolate auction was interesting," said Thad. "I might auction off some chocolate next week. Do you like chocolate all the time, Mitchell? Will you like it next week?"

"Wait a minute. I'm in charge of chocolate," said Henry.

Maggie ate her sardine sandwich and wished it were chocolate.

But she was glad her new column had been delivered safely. In a few days everyone would be reading it and admiring it!

When Maggie got home from school, Mrs. Marmelstein had a big snack waiting for her. "This will make you forget all about cauliflower cookies," she said as she put a large bowl of bread pudding in front of Maggie. "Did everyone shrink from my cauliflower cookies? Did Noah get them?"

"Yes, but he spent all his time eating the peanut butter sandwich. It was like he was in slow motion. So lunch was over before he could eat his dessert."

"His body was working slow but his head was working fast," said Mrs. Marmelstein. "He managed not to eat the cookies."

There was a knock on the door. Mrs. Marmelstein opened it. "Well, hello, my friend Thad Smith. Come in, come in."

Thad walked in. "Hi, Mrs. Marmelstein," he said.

"You're getting to be not a stranger," said Mrs. Marmelstein. "This is the fifth time you've been by this week. And it's only Thursday."

"You're here again?" said Maggie.

"That's not friendly," said Thad.

"Well, you keep asking to see my homework and you want me to write you cards and stuff."

"I came for a friendly visit today."

"How about a friendly visit with Tamara?" said Maggie.

"I'm not friends with Tamara. I told you that," said Thad. "I'm just not enemies with her. There's a big difference."

"I see the difference clearly and distinctly," said Mrs. Marmelstein.

"Besides, you're much smarter than Tamara," Thad added.

"Oh," said Maggie. "Why are you here for the fifth time this week?" Maggie pretended that she was trying to change the subject, but she didn't really want to. She wanted to know exactly how Thad thought she was smarter than Tamara. In school? Out of school? In many ways? In all ways?

But Thad went along with the change of subject. "Well," he said, "I'm writing a letter to a friend and I want to tell him about the weather being wet but warm on Wednesday."

"Wasn't the weather dry and cold on Wednesday?" asked Mrs. Marmelstein. "Wednesday was just yesterday. Yesterday I got nipped by the weather."

"Oh did you?" said Thad. "Well, it must have been the Wednesday before yesterday's Wednesday that was warm and wet."

"I can't recall that Wednesday," said Mrs. Marmelstein.

"Good," said Thad. "I mean, I want to write to

my friend about *that* Wednesday's weather, and I thought that Maggie could print it for me so that it's nice and clear."

"The weather or the way it's printed?" asked Mrs. Marmelstein.

"The way it's printed," said Thad. "Maggie expresses herself well, and this has to be written right. My friend is a weather freak. He has friends all over the country who send him weather reports. And I'm the one who sends them from this area." Thad took a pen and a piece of paper out of his pocket. He handed them to Maggie. "Print," he said.

Maggie took the pen and paper. She printed, "YOU are having a weird day." And she handed the pen and paper back to Thad.

Thad looked at the paper and smiled. "Thanks," he said.

"What do you mean thanks?" asked Maggie. "I didn't print your weather report."

"Oh well," said Thad. "Nothing's perfect. See you later."

"If you do, that would be the sixth time this week," said Mrs. Marmelstein.

After Thad left, Mrs. Marmelstein said, "I'm not sure what that was all about."

"Neither am I," said Maggie.

Thad went into his apartment. "Weird is wonderful," he said to himself. And he called Henry.

18
Keeping Maggie's Secret

Henry rushed over to Thad's house.

"Look at this," said Thad as he held up the paper Maggie had printed on. "Look at the w in weird. Is that a nervous w or is that a nervous w?"

"Highly nervous," said Henry.

Thad put his hand on Henry's shoulder. "Maggie Marmelstein is the Mystery Person."

"I suspected that from the very beginning," said Henry. "If anyone had asked me, I would have said Maggie Marmelstein is my prime suspect."

"Henry, how can you say that? After you tried so hard to prove it was me."

"Well, suspecting you was just a passing thought. It went by so fast I hardly knew I had it. And now that my original suspicion has been proven right, let's do something about it, fast. We've got this hot piece of news, the answer to the biggest question in school."

"We have to keep Maggie's secret," said Thad.

"What? What? Why?" asked Henry. "Now *my* w's are getting nervous. Can you hear my wiggly w's? They're wiggly because I can't believe what you just said. Think of all the praise we'll get. Think of the admiration."

"Maggie is my friend," said Thad.

"You mean we can't tell *anybody*?" said Henry. "I'll die, Thad. I'll die right here, right now. Watch me keel over."

"Well, we can tell one person that we know. Just one person," said Thad.

"Who's that?" asked Henry.

"Maggie Marmelstein," said Thad.

"But she already knows," said Henry.

"Yes, but she doesn't know we know," said Thad.

"That's a minor thrill," said Henry. "Just a very minor thrill."

"Well, if you want to tell everyone, I can't stop you," said Thad. "But I'm not going to do it."

"You know I wouldn't do it without you," said Henry. "What kind of best pal do you think I am? I'm the best best pal. Okay, on to Maggie's apartment."

Henry and Thad walked down the hall.

"Let's do this slowly," said Thad. "Let's save it for the last. We'll talk about other things, and then at the end when it seems like we don't have anything else to say, we'll say it."

"Good strategy," said Henry.

Thad knocked on Maggie's door. Maggie opened it.

"Well, hello there, Mystery Person," said Henry.

19
Ceiling Thoughts

. . . .
****

"What do you mean?" asked Maggie, who knew exactly what Henry meant.

"Should I tell you right here in the hall, or in your apartment?" asked Henry.

"Come in," said Maggie. She hoped she wasn't shaking.

Henry and Thad walked in. "Where's your mother?" asked Thad.

"Watching an old movie on television in the other room," said Maggie.

"Okay, so this is a private conversation among the three of us, right?" said Thad.

"Right!" said Maggie. She didn't know what to say next. Had Henry only been guessing that she was the Mystery Person? The less she said, the better. She would just listen.

"I'm listening to you, Henry," said Maggie.

"I have already spoken," said Henry. "I called you the Mystery Person and that's who you are."

Maggie didn't say anything.

"Well?" said Henry.

"Well, you spoke and I listened, and that's that," said Maggie.

"No, it isn't," said Thad. "I know, too. Henry and I know your secret together."

"What makes you think that's my secret?" asked Maggie. Now Maggie was afraid to speak, and afraid to keep quiet. Her life as the Mystery Person was collapsing.

"Your secret is spread on liver crackers," said Thad.

Henry laughed. "That's funny, Thad."

"Tell me more," said Maggie.

"Tell her what you did, Henry," said Thad. "Tell her the whole story including who you thought was the Mystery Person."

"I'd very much like to leave that part out," said Henry, "and concentrate on my cleverly getting hold of the column from Noah's lunch bag."

"Okay," said Thad. "And I'll take over the story when we get to the nervous w's. That was my contribution to discovering the identity of the Mystery Person."

"Nervous w's?" said Maggie.

"*Your* nervous w's," said Thad. "As in, 'YOU are having a w-e-i-r-d day.' "

"You've been weird all week," said Maggie. "You think I didn't notice?"

"Please, let me tell my story," said Henry.

And while Maggie listened, Henry and then Thad told her how they had found out she was the Mystery Person.

When they finished, Maggie slumped in a chair. "Well, I guess it's all over. It was fun while it lasted but it didn't last very long."

"It's lasting," said Thad. "Henry and I aren't going to tell anybody."

"You're not?" said Maggie. "Why not?"

"Because the secret belongs to you, not me, and Thad Smith doesn't take things that belong to other people," said Thad.

Henry looked puzzled. "I'm trying to figure out what you just said. Didn't you tell me the reason was because Maggie is your friend?"

Thad looked at the ceiling. "Well, I may have said that," he said.

Maggie looked at the ceiling, too. She wished she could share Thad's ceiling thoughts. He was her friend, after all. Even if he didn't want to come out and say so.

20
"Thad Smith
Is Really My Friend."

. . . .
****

Maggie's telephone rang just as Thad and Henry were going out the door. "You're busy today, Maggie," said Henry. "Does the Mystery Person have a busy life, or would you be busy anyway?"

Maggie didn't feel busy, she felt confused. She closed the door. Then she picked up the receiver.

"Maggie, is that you? Noah here. I just read your column about Dipsey Ford."

"Oh?"

"Are you asleep, Maggie? Sorry if I woke you."

"I'm awake."

"Well, some of your column is splendid and some of it isn't splendid."

"Oh?"

"Are you sure you're awake?"

"I'm sure."

"The first part, especially about the plants, is excellent."

"You and my mother are plant people."

"I don't know what you mean," said Noah. "But

the second section, the sad-cheerful part, is too personal. It's like saying that Dipsey has holes in her socks and inviting everyone to help sew them up."

"Noah, this column will help Dipsey just the way my first column helped Ellen," said Maggie.

"I just want you to change the second part of the column. Dipsey doesn't need your help."

"*I'm* the Mystery Person," said Maggie.

"Agreed," said Noah. "But *I'm* your editor."

"No changes," said Maggie. "The Mystery Person has spoken."

"Very well," said Noah. "But I don't think Miss Stemmish will be humming when I turn this in."

"Wait till Tuesday comes around," said Maggie. "And you'll be happy about the whole thing."

"Are you serious? Miss Stemmish and I will be down in the dumps together. Look for us there."

Maggie wondered, "Should I or should I not tell Noah that Thad and Henry found out I'm the Mystery Person? He sounds so unhappy that maybe some more unhappy news won't make any difference. But I could wait until after the Dipsey column comes out. He'll be so glad about that column that even bad news will sound like good news. And it's not even bad news anyway. Because Thad Smith is really my friend."

"Are you still there, Maggie?"

"Yes, and Thad Smith is really my friend," said Maggie.

"Why are you thinking about Thad?" asked Noah. "I sincerely hope you're not planning to help *him* the way you helped Dipsey."

"No, I was just thinking how great everything is."

"You're a very optimistic person, Maggie Marmelstein," said Noah, and he hung up.

Maggie called to her mother, "I have to speak to my invaluable consultant."

Mrs. Marmelstein came into the room. "I'm all ears," she said.

"Well, I have something to tell you that will surprise you. Thad and Henry know I'm the Mystery Person," said Maggie.

"Oh dear," said Mrs. Marmelstein. "Were we done in by liver crackers and cauliflower cookies?"

"It wasn't the food. It was the w's. But that's not important," said Maggie. "See, they're not telling. Thad Smith could have told. He could have been a big star, a famous discoverer. But he'd rather be a friend."

"The Mystery Person brought out the best in Thad Smith," said Mrs. Marmelstein.

"And the best in me, too," said Maggie. "Wait and see."

Maggie started to count the days until Tuesday. "When the Mystery Column is printed, Thad will know *I* wrote it. He'll know and he won't tell. It will be *our* secret!"

21
The Dipsey Disaster

• •

****

Tuesday at school Maggie had to wait her turn to get to a pile of the newspapers.

"Did the Mystery Person write about you?" Mitchell Fritz asked Ronald the Rock Thrower.

"No. I am glad to say that Ronald the Rock Thrower is not in this disaster of a column," said Ronald. "It's a Dipsey disaster."

Maggie smiled. Ronald was always making bad jokes. She picked up a copy of the newspaper. There was her column, just as she had written it. It looked spectacular.

"Hey, Dipsey, how lucky can you get?" said Jody Klinger. "The Mystery Person wrote about *you*! On second thought—make that unlucky. This is awful."

Maggie watched as Dipsey Ford picked up a newspaper and read the Mystery Person column. Her face turned from sad to desperate. "Yuck!" she said.

"Just think about the plant and flute parts," said Ellen. "They're really very nice."

Dipsey looked as if she were about to cry.

"I've got a big joke for you, Dipsey, and a little

tickle, too," said Ronald. "Let's see you look at least one-half happy."

"Oh, be quiet, Ronald," said Jody.

Maggie walked away. Ronald was stupid! "Everyone knows Dipsey needs help," Maggie thought. "So I just reminded them. Dipsey will be glad about the column after the shock wears off."

"Hey, Dipsey, did you hear the joke about the chicken who always wore yellow underwear but nobody could tell!" Someone was yelling at Dipsey.

Maggie saw Thad reading the newspaper. He looked down at the paper and then up at Maggie and then down at the paper. Then he said, "This column could be a lot better. Somebody should tell that to the Mystery Person."

Suddenly Maggie felt like running away. Tamara rushed up. "Have you seen the Mystery Person column? It's so dumb. And I predict that the column is going to get worse and worse."

"I predict it isn't," said Maggie.

"How would *you* know?" asked Tamara.

"I'm good at predictions," said Maggie.

"It *will* be better," said Thad. "I'm good at predictions, too." Then he walked away.

Maggie wished the day were over. She tried not to listen when kids talked about the Mystery Person column. She especially tried not to listen when they told terrible jokes to Dipsey Ford. Maggie and Noah exchanged looks as usual, but now she wondered what Noah's look meant.

When Maggie got home from school, her telephone was ringing. "Noah's on the phone," Mrs. Marmelstein said before she answered it. She picked up the receiver. "Hello, Noah Moore. Your timing is once again perfection. Here's Maggie."

"Hi, Noah." Maggie spoke into the receiver. "Before you say anything, I want to say that the Mystery Person won't be giving out help any longer. So let's not talk about the Dipsey column."

"I'm glad to hear that," said Noah. "So now we can just talk about some exciting news I have. Your first fan letter has arrived. About an hour after the newspaper came out, someone left an envelope addressed to the Mystery Person in the school office. Naturally it was turned over to me. I'll put it in my lunch bag Thursday, so when we exchange bags, you'll get the letter. I didn't open the envelope, so I don't know what the letter says."

"Suspense!" said Maggie.

"Of the highest order," said Noah. "And speaking of suspense, I'm wondering who will be the subject of your next column."

"You'll find out in your lunch bag," said Maggie.

"But, Maggie, considering the problems with the Dipsey column, I'd really like . . ."

"We're not talking about the Dipsey column, remember? You can trust the Mystery Person to use her power wisely now."

"Power," said Noah. *"Power?"*

Maggie was thinking, "Is this or is this not a good time to tell Noah that Thad and Henry know I'm the Mystery Person? It is not. After my next wonderful column, that's when I'll tell Noah."

After Maggie hung up, her mother said, "I guess I won't ask about the Dipsey column that we're not supposed to talk about."

Maggie took some milk and Mystery Muffins.

Then she said, "Dipsey got lots of attention. Actually she got too much attention. And she looked sadder than ever. So now I'm wiser than ever."

"And I'm confused," said Mrs. Marmelstein.

"Well, now I know the Mystery Person is just supposed to write wonderful columns that kids are crazy about reading. And that's it. Straight facts. No advice. No help. And now I'm going to write my most wonderful column ever."

"Nicely fortified by Mystery Muffins," said Mrs. Marmelstein.

Maggie finished eating and went to her room. She sat down at her desk. "This will be my most wonderful column because I'm going to write about Noah."

Maggie wrote:

```
Today's column is about Noah
Moore. Noah is the smartest
kid in school. Noah doesn't
```

need any help at all and if he
did, I, the Mystery Person,
would not give it to him.
   Noah is president of the
sixth grade and editor of this
newspaper and most likely a
future president of the United
States. Noah is very kind, and
if you visit him when he is
president, he will probably
invite you into his rose
garden and give you some
roses to take home with you.
   Noah does not take part in
sports, but if he did, we all
know he would be great in
whatever he took part in.
              Mysteriously Yours,
              The Mystery Person

Maggie rushed into the kitchen with her column.
"Read this," she said to her mother.

Mrs. Marmelstein wiped some crumbs off her fingers
and read the column. "I'm a mixed person about it,"
she said. "The column truly describes Noah, but Noah
wouldn't want to be truly described in his own newspaper. It will seem like he's advertising himself."

"I can fix that," said Maggie. "I'll say in the column
that Noah has to print whatever the Mystery Person
writes because it's the Mystery Person's column. And
that he's not connected with it. Like 'No resemblance

to persons living or dead,' or something like that. Which is what they put in books."

"I don't think that's the same thing," said Mrs. Marmelstein. "But ask him if he wants to be in your column. And maybe leave out about no connections or resemblance to the living or dead."

"I'm not going to ask him," said Maggie, "because it's *my* column. Besides, Noah is too modest."

"That's part of being Noah," said Mrs. Marmelstein. "Noah wouldn't want himself printed."

"Well, he's going to be. I'll just stick this column in my lunch bag Thursday. It will be a fun swap because Noah's got something for me. The Mystery Person's first fan letter came. Noah has it and he's putting it in his lunch bag for me on Thursday. He hasn't read it because it's for me."

"Well, you asked your readers to write to you, so now you'll find out what one of them thinks of your column," said Mrs. Marmelstein. "One opinion. It's not exactly the Gallup poll, but it should be interesting."

22
The Double Swap

On Thursday Maggie put her Noah column in a lunch bag along with an egg salad sandwich and a piece of coconut cake.

Mrs. Marmelstein said, "Your invaluable consultant says that you can't take liver crackers and cauliflower cookies anymore. Today you should have a regular unsuspicious lunch. Everyone will still think it's irregular because of your past record. By the time they find out it's regular, Noah will have it. Remember, no advance announcements about the contents. A bad reputation is something you can depend upon, even in lunch bags."

Maggie felt jittery. This would be a double swap. She had something for Noah. Noah had something for her. She knew Thad and Henry would be watching. And Tamara would be there, too. She was sure of it.

At lunch Maggie sat down as soon as she could, and then she stood up as soon as she could. She wanted to get everything over with.

"I have a delectable lunch today," she said, holding up her bag.

Thad and Henry looked at her and smiled.

"Broken record, broken record," yelled Ronald. "That's what you said last time."

"And today I have my classic Noah Moore basic lunch," said Noah. "Tuna fish on rye, three marshmallows and a can of fruit punch."

"Ho hum," said Ronald.

"Boring, boring," said Dipsey Ford.

"I accept your bid," Maggie said to Noah.

"Wait. I haven't bid," said Noah. "I now bid my entire lunch for your entire lunch."

"Sold to the highest bidder," said Maggie, and she sat down.

Henry and Thad started kicking each other under the table.

Noah got up, walked to where Maggie was sitting, and was about to swap lunch bags with her when he heard a voice shout, "Stop!"

Maggie and Noah turned around. Tamara was smiling at them. She said, "I want to bid on Maggie's delectable, delectable lunch."

"Too late," Maggie said. "The bidding is closed."

"But look what *I* have to bid," said Tamara as she held up a huge, bulging bag.

"Wow!" said Mitchell Fritz.

"For openers," said Tamara, "I have miniature pizza squares, still warm, thanks to a special heating technique developed by my aunt, a prominent nutritionist."

"Take them, take them, Maggie," said Jody Klinger.

Tamara continued. "I also have a thermos of hot chocolate, in case you're cold, and a thermos of chilled chocolate milk, in case you're hot."

"I'm medium," said Maggie.

"Medium? How perfect," said Tamara. "For medium, I have brownies with chopped walnuts, neither hot nor cold."

"I want them! I want them!" yelled Ronald. "I'll swap my aunt for your aunt, Tamara, if you give me your lunch."

Tamara reached deep into her bag. "I also have . . ." she started to say.

"Take Tamara's lunch, Maggie!" yelled Mitchell Fritz.

"Take it! Take it!" yelled Jody.

Everyone except Henry, Thad, and Noah started to chant, "Take Tamara's lunch! Take Tamara's lunch!"

The next table took up the chant.

Maggie looked at Noah. She wondered if she looked as terrified as he did. She *couldn't* give her lunch bag, with the Mystery Person column in it, to Tamara! But how could she get out of it? Everyone knew that Tamara's lunch was better than Noah's.

Thad spoke up. "Pizza can give a person a stomachache. It can burn a person's tongue. It can . . ."

Everyone kept on chanting.

Noah said, "I believe there are rules governing auctions. These rules are well documented and rather inflexible. Tamara has broken at least two of them.

The bidding was closed before she started. Further-more . . ." Noah was speaking as loud as he could. But no one was listening. They were still chanting. At last Noah gave up.

Now Maggie knew she would have to swap lunch bags with Tamara! The identity of the Mystery Person was about to be revealed.

Maggie glared at Tamara as she handed her the lunch bag. Tamara smiled broadly as she handed her lunch bag to Maggie. The bag felt like a sack of rocks to Maggie. Maggie looked quickly inside in the hope that Tamara had actually packed rocks in there, and that Maggie could get her own lunch bag back. But inside Tamara's bag was all the tempting food she had de-scribed, and more. Tamara had come well prepared. And now she had Maggie's lunch bag in her hands. She sat down.

Maggie and Noah waited anxiously for her to open the bag. But instead Tamara put it in her lap. She made rustling, crunching noises with the bag, under the table. But she didn't even look inside.

"I guess I just don't feel like liver crackers or cauli-flower cookies today," she announced.

"You did one minute ago," said Ronald.

"I want to swap back," said Tamara, putting the bag on the table.

Maggie and Noah exchanged puzzled looks. Then Maggie grabbed her lunch bag and handed Tamara's back to her. Quickly, Maggie and Noah exchanged their lunch bags. Maggie could hardly believe that her lunch bag was now safely in Noah's hands.

Noah said to Tamara, "You didn't even *want* Maggie's lunch. You simply wanted to show everyone you could get it. And look! It's a nice egg salad sandwich and coconut cake."

"It was normal and you missed out on it, Tamara!" yelled Ronald.

"Hear, hear!" cried Mitchell Fritz. "Never make a deal with Tamara Axelrod!"

"Poor sport, poor sport!" yelled Ronald. "I'm glad I didn't swap aunts. I might have gotten mine back."

Tamara smiled. She didn't look bothered at all. She cheerfully passed a few pizza squares around the table, and everyone settled down to eat.

Toward the end of lunch Maggie said, "I'm full. I can't eat another bite. So I'll just save some of my lunch for later."

Noah didn't say anything, but once again he tucked his lunch bag between two books. It had been decided in advance that this time Maggie would be the one to make the comment about saving part of lunch for later. "I'm already known as a saver," Noah had said. Now Maggie put her lunch bag between two books. Their plan had worked once more. Noah had his column and Maggie had her fan letter. She would read it when she got home.

As Maggie was leaving school at the end of the day, Noah came up to her and whispered, "Maggie, I know we're not supposed to whisper together or huddle together or look conspiratorial, but I'm absolutely elated that we managed our lunch bag exchange today. We triumphed under the most adverse conditions."

"I'm still shaking," said Maggie. "At least I think I'm shaking."

"Don't shake," said Noah. "*Soar*, as Miss Stemmish would say. I have the column and you have the fan letter. Now let's run home, read what we have and call one another up. Cheers!"

Noah dashed off down the street. Maggie stood there and watched him. She wanted to believe that everything had worked out well. But somehow she couldn't.

23
"A Few Sprinkles,
but Not Too Much."

• •
✻✻✻✻✻✻✻✻✻✻✻✻✻✻✻✻✻✻✻✻✻✻✻✻✻✻✻✻✻✻✻✻✻✻✻✻✻✻✻

When Maggie got home, her mother was on the telephone. "Right on time," Mrs. Marmelstein said as she handed the receiver to Maggie. "It's Noah, but he doesn't sound like Noah," Mrs. Marmelstein whispered.

"Hello," said Maggie. "Are you Noah? My mother says you don't sound like Noah."

"Oh dear," said Mrs. Marmelstein.

"I'm Noah and I've just read your column," said Noah. "I have a lot to say."

"Wait till I open my fan letter," said Maggie, "so I can have a lot to say, too." Maggie took the envelope from her lunch bag and looked at it. It was marked: TO THE MYSTERY PERSON. She opened it. There was a piece of paper inside. She read from it into the telephone:

DEAR MYSTERY PERSON,
YOUR COLUMN IS THE PITS.
        YOURS TRULY,
        RONALD THE ROCK THROWER

"I might have known," said Noah. "But at least he cared enough to write."

"I suppose so," said Maggie. "Now what did you want to tell me? How do you like my new column?"

"I hate it," said Noah. "And I refuse to print it. So could you please write another column very quickly? In fact immediately. So I can hand it in to Miss Stemmish tomorrow morning."

"Noah, you're so modest!"

"What do you mean, Maggie?"

"You know what I mean. This is a good column."

"Maggie, this column is worse than your last column and you know how that one turned out."

"Noah, I'm the Mystery Person and I've decided that this column is going to be printed. So good-bye and enjoy it, and I know you will."

Noah hung up.

Maggie wondered if Noah had forgotten to say good-bye, or whether he had forgotten on purpose.

She went to the refrigerator, got some milk, and poured it into a glass. She sat down and started to drink it. "Is the milk sour?" asked Mrs. Marmelstein. "Your face says so."

"I had a fight with Noah," said Maggie. "Over the column."

"I heard your end of the conversation," said Mrs. Marmelstein. "He didn't like the column, did he?" Mrs. Marmelstein sat down beside Maggie.

"He hates it. He doesn't want to print it," said Maggie. "But I told him he had to because it's my column."

Mrs. Marmelstein scratched her head. "Are you in the mood for some invaluable consulting?"

Maggie gulped down her milk. "I don't think so," she said.

"Then how about one question? Just one question for Maggie to ask Maggie. What's more important—the column or Noah's feelings?" said Mrs. Marmelstein.

Maggie didn't answer. She was thinking about Noah. She was thinking about Dipsey Ford and the terrible jokes about a chicken's underwear. And she was thinking about Thad Smith. The Mystery Person business *had* brought out the best in Thad. What had it brought out in her?

Then she said, "Thad Smith let me keep my column and my power. But now I'm not sure I want it. I don't think I like the Mystery Person anymore. I like Maggie Marmelstein better. But we're the same person. Or are we?"

"Thad Smith knew what to do with power," said Mrs. Marmelstein. "He dumped it."

"Do you think I should dump mine?" asked Maggie.

"That's a Maggie decision," said Mrs. Marmelstein. "What do *you* think?"

"Maybe power should be passed from person to person," said Maggie. "And no one should keep it too long."

"Like salt and sugar," said Mrs. Marmelstein. "A

few sprinkles, but not too much. Pass the power. Your invaluable consultant likes that idea."

Maggie kissed her mother. "The Mystery Person and Maggie Marmelstein have a lot of thinking to do," she said.

Maggie went to her room. She sat by her telephone. She wondered what Noah was doing and thinking at this very moment.

Noah sat by his telephone for half an hour after he had finished talking with Maggie. He was hoping she would call back. "Perhaps I did wrong in selecting Maggie as the Mystery Person," he thought. "Perhaps *I* changed her from perfectly sane Maggie Marmelstein into someone with perfectly terrible judgment. I can forgive her rather rousing temper—it rounds out her personality—but I fear her judgment has totally collapsed. Why else would Maggie write this stupid column and want it published!"

Noah read the column again:

```
Today's column is about two
kids, Tamara Axelrod and Thad
Smith. When I think of one, I
think of the other. That's how
much Thad and Tamara are
together. They have the same
first initial. But that's not
the only same they have. Some
```

other sames are that they like
the same sports and food.
Hobbies, too. There is a long
list of sames. If you want to
find out anything more about
Thad, ask Tamara. If you want
to find out anything more
about Tamara, ask Thad. It
will be very easy to ask these
questions because you will
probably see Thad and Tamara
together at the same time.
Maggie Marmelstein is very
sorry about this, but she
knows it's true.

Mysteriously Yours,
The Mystery Person

24
A Phony Column

The next morning Noah walked into Miss Stemmish's office. He handed her all the columns for next week's newspaper.

"You're right on time as usual, Noah," said Miss Stemmish.

Noah wasn't in the mood to exchange their regular conversation. He was angry about the Mystery Person column.

"You won't like me today, Miss Stemmish," he said. "Today I am thoroughly unlikable."

"Impossible," said Miss Stemmish. "It's simply early-morning depression. It will lift. It will soar away. I'll just go photocopy these columns. Then I'll be back and I know I'll see your usual good-natured self."

Miss Stemmish walked off with the columns. She was gone for fifteen minutes. "There was a long line at the photocopy machine," she explained when she returned. "A strange assortment of copies today. Two valentines, a certificate of honor for a dog. I didn't mean to peek, but . . ."

"I understand," said Noah. "Lines are so boring that

one is tempted to peek in front and in back of oneself. An active mind can't be confined in a line, you know."

"How eloquent," said Miss Stemmish. She handed the columns back to Noah. "I'm anxious to read the Mystery Person column," she said.

"Don't be," said Noah. "I don't want to print it but I have to. The Mystery Person insists. Well, I hope I haven't spoiled your day. Forget about me, and have a good one, Miss Stemmish."

"You'll be soaring soon, Noah," said Miss Stemmish.

"Sinking, Miss Stemmish. All day long."

Noah dragged himself through the day. Maggie looked as if she wanted to say something to him, but she didn't say anything.

"I imagine that I look like I want to say something to Maggie," thought Noah. But he didn't say anything.

On the way home from school, Thad caught up with Noah. "All hail the wiggly w," said Thad.

"What wiggly w?" asked Noah.

"You mean Maggie didn't tell you?" asked Thad.

"Tell me what?" asked Noah.

"Well, never mind," said Thad.

"I *do* mind," said Noah. "Notice that I'm in my sinking mood. I mind everything. Please tell me about wiggly w."

"Well, okay," said Thad. "Henry hogs the story when he tells it, anyway."

Noah and Thad walked on slowly while Thad told Noah just how he and Henry learned the identity of the Mystery Person. "But we're not telling anyone," said Thad. "So you won't be sinking any lower, will you?"

"Definitely not," said Noah. "I'm impressed."

"Do you think Maggie is, too?" asked Thad. "I'm not sure."

Suddenly Noah stopped walking. "That's it! That's it!" he said. "You thought of something I didn't think of. You noticed something I didn't notice. You are so much smarter than I am."

"I am?" said Thad. "Boy, is that news. Could you put it in headlines in your newspaper? *Thad Smith smarter than Noah Moore.* Three inches high with a dark border around it. Print a few extras. I want to send copies to my relatives out west. Maybe you could write a little story to go with it."

"That would certainly be a better column than the one I handed in today," said Noah. "I must show you something, Thad."

"Sure," said Thad. "I'm beginning to feel important. Should I?"

"By all means," said Noah. "You might be the key person to help Maggie Marmelstein and me."

"Sometimes Maggie wants my help and sometimes she doesn't," said Thad.

"Maggie says that you're really her friend," said Noah.

"She doesn't say that all the time," said Thad. "I can tell you plenty of times that she didn't say that.

There was a whole week once, and then a Tuesday, and a couple of holidays, and the month of May, many mornings, and remember frog time?"

Noah didn't answer. He was fishing in his books for his columns. "Music, current events, editorial, oh here it is, the newest Mystery Person column." Noah handed the column to Thad. "Read," he said.

Thad glanced down at the column. "Is this a bad joke? This *is* a bad joke."

"It's Maggie's latest column," said Noah.

"No it isn't," said Thad. "Maggie didn't print this. It's a forgery. A phony."

"But you only glanced at it," said Noah. "That's not very thorough or conclusive."

"It is when there aren't any nervous w's," said Thad. "See, Maggie's w's are always nervous. Wiggly, sort of. Someone must have copied her printing, but they didn't bother to wiggle their w's. The rest of the printing *does* look like Maggie's. No wonder you thought it was. Somebody went to a lot of trouble to imitate Maggie's printing."

"That's exactly what I thought you'd say," said Noah. "When I read it, it never occurred to me that Maggie didn't write this column. But after you told me your wiggly w story, I realized that I hadn't examined the printing or even thought to do it. Thad, *someone* figured out that Maggie is the Mystery Person and imitated her printing, hoping to get this phony column published."

"But how could anyone get a sample of Maggie's printing? It's almost impossible to do that, believe me."

"No, it isn't," said Noah. "Maggie is forever making notes in school and throwing them in wastebaskets."

"Wastebaskets!" said Thad. "And I was going crazy with wish, wonderful, week, weather, wet, warm, and Wednesday. If it weren't for weird, I'd still be looking."

Noah went on. "Our someone figured out that Maggie's columns could be in the lunch bags she gave me. So someone took Maggie's column from the bag yesterday and substituted this one about you and Tamara that the someone had printed in advance." Noah looked puzzled. "But how did the column get switched? Nobody got into my lunch bag yesterday. There wasn't a fainter in sight."

"Back up," said Thad. "Why would this person suspect that the column was in the lunch bag anyway?"

"Because Henry fished a supposedly empty lunch bag out of the trash can," said Noah. "The bag was covered with all kinds of unmentionable guck. But Henry gave it back to me and I accepted it. A lot of kids saw me take it. I tried to explain it away, but the bag looked thoroughly disgusting. *Deceased*, actually. Why would I take it back? I knew why and Henry knew why. There was something of value in the lunch bag. I should have realized at the time how highly suspicious my actions were. Henry's, too. I imagine our unknown someone briefly thought that Henry might be the Mystery Person."

"Henry?" said Thad. "Nobody could think *that!*"

"Maybe not," said Noah. "Because they don't know that Henry writes very well. In fact, he was runner-up for Mystery Person."

"*What?*" said Thad. "Watch out. *I'm* going to faint on you, Noah."

"Henry's entry contained a variety of writings," said Noah. "Two lines of this, two lines of that. Very dizzying. Variety did in Henry."

"Runner-up, huh?" said Thad.

"Let's get back to the lunch bag," said Noah. "It *came* from Maggie. It had *belonged* to Maggie."

"So your unknown person figured out that Maggie Marmelstein could have put something in that bag, like a Mystery Person column," said Thad.

"Yes," said Noah. "I wonder whom Maggie really wrote about in her third column. Well, I'll soon find out. I'm going to her house right now. I'm afraid I must show her this column."

"Maggie's house is my house, too," said Thad. "So I'll go with you."

"Into Maggie's apartment?" asked Noah.

"Are you kidding?" said Thad. "I'll come over much later. After you show her this column. After she's through being furious about it. I'm a coward, Noah."

"As a matter of fact, so am I," said Noah. "Say, how brave is Henry?"

"Not *that* brave," said Thad.

25
A Crackly
and Crinkly Maneuver

"I didn't write this!" Maggie Marmelstein almost screamed.

"I know it, I know it," said Noah. "But I didn't know it yesterday. You and I were talking about two different columns and we didn't know it."

"Maybe 'Shh' isn't the best communication system," said Mrs. Marmelstein.

Noah looked at his watch. "It's 3:55. Miss Stemmish is on her tea and scones. She'll be taking the columns to the printer's at four. We must stop her. We need a column fast to replace this one. I can read the new column over the phone and Miss Stemmish can type it up."

"But I don't have any column," said Maggie. "I don't even have a copy of the column *I* wrote. And I'm not fast enough to write a new column in five minutes."

"Then we'll have no Mystery Person column to print," said Noah. "The Mystery Person column will be a blank unless . . ."

"Unless what?" asked Maggie.

Noah looked directly at Maggie. "We're desperate, right?"

"Right," said Maggie.

"Do you feel bold and full of courage? Like a real columnist?"

"I *am* a real columnist," said Maggie. "I'm part of the newspaper business."

"So you can take public criticism whether it's justified or not?" asked Noah.

"A *real* columnist can, so I can," said Maggie.

"Good," said Noah. "Then I think we have a column. Listen!"

And Noah explained his column idea to Maggie.

"We've got guts," said Maggie. And they both started to write. Mrs. Marmelstein served cocoa. "To fortify your guts."

Five minutes later Noah telephoned Miss Stemmish. "Hello," she said. She sounded as if her mouth were full of scones.

"Miss Stemmish," Noah said, "I want to replace the Mystery Person column I gave you with another column. Now take this down, please."

"Just a minute," said Miss Stemmish. "Let me wash your column down with one last sip of tea." There was a long pause and then Miss Stemmish said, "Ready."

Noah slowly dictated the column that he and Maggie had decided upon.

"Oh, this is raw, lean journalism!" said Miss Stemmish. "I'm simply enthralled. The principal loves raw, lean journalism. I'll type this up right away. I didn't like that third Mystery Person column anyway."

Miss Stemmish was expressing more and more opinions. Noah was glad. "Fine, Miss Stemmish," he said. And he hung up.

Noah turned to Maggie. "Your third column will be off to the printer's as soon as the scones and tea are digested. Now, I'm curious. Who was the subject of your first third column?"

"You," said Maggie.

"Me?" said Noah. "But why, Maggie? I wouldn't want a column about me in my own newspaper."

"That's what my invaluable consultant said," said Maggie. "But I wasn't listening."

There was a knock at the door and Henry and Thad walked in. "For the sixth time lately, hello, Mrs. Marmelstein," said Thad. Then he asked, "Has Maggie seen the column?"

Noah and Mrs. Marmelstein nodded.

Thad turned to Maggie. "Somebody is out to get you and your column. I came over to help you, and Henry came over to help me help you."

"Thanks," said Maggie. It felt strange saying thanks to Thad. But it also felt great.

Henry looked down at the column.

"I bet I know who wrote this," he said.

"I bet I know who wrote this," said Thad.

"I bet I know who wrote this," said Maggie.

"I see I have no one to bet with," said Noah. "We're all thinking of the same person."

"Tamara Axelrod," said Mrs. Marmelstein. "Your invaluable consultant also has no one to bet with."

"I should have known immediately," said Noah. "But I thought our column was inviolate."

"What does that mean?" asked Thad.

"It means he didn't think Tamara Axelrod could get her grimy hands on it," said Henry.

"Why, that's exactly right, Henry," said Noah.

"Lucky guess," said Henry. "Miss Stemmish once assigned the word, but I forgot to look it up."

Maggie looked at Thad. "You think Tamara would do this? Your pal Tamara?"

"She isn't my pal. I told you that," said Thad. "We're not enemies, that's all. Except now maybe we are."

Maggie was sorry that she was glad to hear Thad say that.

"Tamara even asked me to help her find out who the Mystery Person is," said Thad. "But I never told her about the wiggly w's or anything."

"But how did Tamara switch columns?" asked Henry. "I didn't see her faint."

"Let's think," said Mrs. Marmelstein. "Where was the column from the moment it left here in Maggie's lunch bag?"

"I went straight to school with it," said Maggie. "I clutched it from class to class. I had it all the time until I swapped it with Noah's bag."

Thad piped up. "Hey, no you didn't. *Tamara* got the bag when she made the highest bid. Remember?"

"Yes," said Noah. "But that was very brief."

"But very crackly and crinkly," said Maggie. "Tamara must have switched columns while she was holding the bag under the table."

"Then Tamara *knows* Maggie is the Mystery Person," said Noah. "And she's not saying anything because she wants to get *her* column printed. But when she finds out that we've caught on to her, she'll reveal that Maggie is the Mystery Person. And if I know her, she'll make a grand announcement. She'll probably put a notice on the bulletin board to invite kids to her grand announcement."

"I bet she serves refreshments made by some relative who's a famous chef," said Henry.

"I'm afraid you're not going to be the Mystery Person much longer, Maggie," said Noah. "Tamara is going to shout your secret."

"No, she isn't," said Maggie.

"But she *knows*," said Noah. "And she'll *tell*."

"She'll be too late," said Maggie. "Because there'll be two tellers before her."

"Whom do you have in mind, Maggie?" asked Noah.

Maggie turned toward Thad and Henry. "You two do it," she said.

"Well, if you really want us to, Maggie," said Thad a little sadly.

Henry didn't look quite so sad.

"I'm passing the power to you," said Maggie.

"It's just a few sprinkles," said Mrs. Marmelstein. "I'm sure that both of you can handle it nicely."

"But what about you, Maggie?" asked Thad. "You'll be through as the Mystery Person."

"I know," said Maggie. "I feel kind of . . ."

"Maybe mixed?" said Mrs. Marmelstein.

"Yes, mixed," said Maggie. "I wanted it to last, but maybe it shouldn't last too long. You can get big ideas being the Mystery Person, and they get bigger and bigger. But I only had two columns. Just two."

"Three," said Noah. "How could you forget next Tuesday's column? It could be your finest hour."

"Yeah, because you're not printing Tamara's column," said Henry.

"That's not what I mean," said Noah. "On Tuesday Maggie's column will be a shining example of raw, lean journalism."

"You sound like Miss Stemmish," said Henry.

"But Tamara will find out on Tuesday that we've found her out," said Thad.

"No, it won't happen that way," said Noah, "because I have a Monday plan. On Monday we'll have another lunch bag auction."

"Why?" asked Maggie. "What are we going to swap? I won't have a column."

"Yes, you will," said Noah. "And I'm sure Tamara

will bid for your lunch again. Because she'll be curious why I'm bidding on your lunch on Monday. She only expects that on Thursdays. But I'll lose. Take Tamara's offer, Maggie."

"If you say so, Noah," said Maggie.

26

"The Mystery Person Is . . ."

• •
****

Maggie didn't sleep well Sunday night. She knew it would be her last night as the Mystery Person. At lunch the next day she would lose her mystery, her column, her power.

"I'm just about back to being one person," she told her mother at breakfast. "By the time lunch is over, everyone will know that I, Maggie Marmelstein, *was* the Mystery Person. Somebody else will be the new one."

"But you'll always be the first," said Mrs. Marmelstein. "The honor is yours forever. Everyone remembers the first of something. Like George Washington. Remember Millard Fillmore? He was number thirteen. Much harder to remember than George Washington." Mrs. Marmelstein started to scramble some eggs. "Besides, the best part of this will never be over, Maggie."

"The best part?" asked Maggie.

"Like finding out how much Thad Smith is really your friend," said Mrs. Marmelstein. "And Henry and Noah, too. Thad and Henry kept your secret, and Noah selected and protected you. And I saw all of you sitting at this very table talking and planning with great relish. That foursome has flavor, I said to myself. Permanent flavor, Maggie. That kind of flavor lasts. Believe me. These are my last few hours as invaluable consultant."

"Oh, you were more than that," said Maggie. "Don't forget your turnip sandwiches and liver crackers and cauliflower cookies." Then Maggie added, "But today I have the best lunch of all."

Maggie ate her breakfast and started off to school.

"Hearty appetite for whatever you land up with," called Mrs. Marmelstein.

Maggie felt that everyone was watching her as she walked around school with her books and her lunch bag. She felt nervous about what was going to happen at lunchtime. Would Noah's plan work? Would something go wrong?

At noon Maggie, Noah, Thad, and Henry walked into the lunchroom together and sat down at a table. Ronald the Rock Thrower joined them, and Ellen, Mitchell Fritz, Jody Klinger, Dipsey Ford, and some others. Tamara came along and pretended she was trying to decide which table to sit at. Then she sat down opposite Maggie.

Maggie waited until everyone was seated. She wanted to wait longer. She wanted to wait forever. She felt as if she were about to speak to an auditorium full of people instead of a bunch of kids at a lunch table.

And she didn't have to give a speech. She only had to auction off her lunch.

"Big deal," thought Maggie. But it *was* a big deal.

Kids were starting to eat. In a minute it would be too late to start an auction. Noah looked at her. He did something stern with his forehead.

Maggie held up her lunch bag. "You will never guess what I have in here today," she said.

"Yes, we will," said Ronald. "A turnip sandwich or four liver crackers or cauliflower cookies. I'm falling asleep. Snore snore."

"Perhaps Ronald guessed right," said Maggie. "An encore treat. In answer to popular demand."

Ellen whispered to Maggie, "I don't think it was very popular, Maggie. And there was hardly any demand."

Maggie smiled weakly at Ellen.

Tamara said, "How come you're auctioning today, Maggie? Isn't Thursday your big auction day?"

Maggie glanced at Noah. Was Tamara suspicious?

"I want it! I want it!" yelled Ronald. "I want to know what an insane lunch tastes like. I have a thermos of tomato soup, an orange, and a graham cracker. It may be plain, but it isn't crazy. You're lucky to have this offer, Maggie."

Noah stood up. "I would like to bid for Maggie's lunch."

"What do you have?" Maggie was afraid her voice sounded forced and rehearsed.

"A hard-boiled-egg sandwich with mayonnaise and lettuce. Several vanilla cookies, one containing a pecan in the middle, and nothing to drink."

"I'm quite thirsty today," said Maggie. She was stalling for time. Why wasn't Tamara bidding? Tamara had a puzzled look on her face, but she didn't say anything more.

"My tomato soup will unthirst you," said Ronald.

Dipsey said, "Take Ronald's offer."

"No, go with the vanilla cookie with one pecan," yelled Mitchell Fritz. "And take a big slurp of water from the water fountain."

Maggie hesitated. The plan was failing. She would *have* to accept Noah's bid.

"I'll bid for your lunch, Maggie," said Tamara.

There it was! Tamara had made her bid!

"Aren't you going to ask me what I have?" said Tamara.

Maggie just couldn't believe it had happened.

"A lovely Swiss cheese sandwich and two saltines."

Tamara hadn't come prepared with a great lunch to swap.

Kids started to yell, "Take Noah's, take Ronald's."

"Swiss cheese and saltines will make you *more* thirsty," Ellen said to Maggie. She was really trying to be helpful.

"I pick Tamara's lunch," said Maggie. "Tamara is the highest bidder."

Tamara looked shocked. She had expected Maggie to try very hard to swap with Noah. Tamara had been about to throw in two pencils, some notebook paper and her favorite zippered pencil pouch with pictures of planets on it in order to get Maggie's lunch bag. Now Maggie was handing it to her.

Tamara handed her lunch bag to Maggie. Maggie took out the cheese sandwich and the crackers. Tamara put Maggie's bag under the table and fished inside. She felt a piece of paper, nothing else. What was going on?

Everyone was eating but Tamara. "Hey, you starving today, Tamara?" asked Ronald.

"My appetite simply comes and simply goes," said Tamara. "I'm waiting for it to appear."

"Appear, appetite!" Ronald yelled.

Tamara sat, holding the lunch bag in her lap. What was on the paper inside of it? Had Maggie given it to her on purpose?

Tamara looked down and slowly pulled part of the paper out of the bag. She started to read it to herself: Today's column is about two kids, Tamara Axelrod and Thad Smith. Tamara quickly shoved the paper back into the bag. It *had* been a trap. Maggie knew that Tamara had written the column. And now she was returning it to Tamara. In public.

"Whatcha doing there, Tamara?" asked Ronald. "Playing hide-and-seek with your lunch? Give it to me. Share your food with the needy." Ronald reached for Tamara's lunch bag.

Tamara held tightly to the bag.

Ronald said, "I'm so needy I can't stand it." And he grabbed the bag. "This sure feels like a light lunch," he said. "What's this? A piece of paper? Is that what you eat for lunch, Maggie? I'm not *that* needy." Ronald tossed the paper into the air. Then he caught it and looked at it. "Hey, listen to this, everybody." Ronald read:

"Today's column is about two kids, Tamara Axelrod and Thad Smith. When I think of one, I think of the other. That's how much Thad and Tamara are together. They have the same first initial. But that's not the only same they have. Some other sames are that they like the same sports and food. Hobbies, too. There is a long list of sames. If you want to find out anything more about Thad, ask Tamara. If you want to find out anything more about Tamara, ask Thad. It will be very easy to ask these questions because you will probably see Thad and Tamara together at the same time.

Maggie Marmelstein is very
sorry about this, but she
knows it's true.
                Mysteriously Yours,
                The Mystery Person
"The above was written by
Tamara Axelrod, who is not the
Mystery Person, and placed in
Noah Moore's lunch bag last
Thursday. It is now being
returned to Tamara Axelrod."

Ronald waved the paper. "What silly mush!" he
yelled. "I have here Tamara Axelrod's silly mush. Who
wants to bid on it? What am I offered for this junk?"

"Give that back to me, Ronald!" said Tamara.

But Ronald held on to the paper.

Everyone at the table started to giggle, and stare
at Tamara. Tamara was squirming. She was thinking,
"Maggie thinks she's won but she hasn't. Because *I'm*
the only one who knows she's the Mystery Person,
and *I'm* going to announce it."

Tamara stood up.

Noah stood up.

Thad stood up.

Henry stood up.

Maggie stood up.

Tamara said, "My uncle and three cousins were all
outstanding detectives. That's why none of you will
be surprised that I'm the only one in this entire school

to discover and now reveal the identity of the Mystery Person."

Henry said, "The Mystery Person is Maggie Marmelstein."

Thad said, "The Mystery Person is Maggie Marmelstein."

Noah said, "The Mystery Person is Maggie Marmelstein, and I should know."

Maggie said, "The Mystery Person is me, and I should know, too."

Tamara stood there with her mouth open and her moment of glory snatched from her.

Ronald applauded. "Everybody do that again. I like to watch Tamara's mouth hang open."

Maggie was full of emotion. She was sorry that her identity had to be revealed, but she was glad that Thad and Henry had done the revealing.

A little crowd started to gather around Maggie's table.

Ronald yelled, "Say something, Mystery Person!"

Maggie said, "Yes, I'm the Mystery Person and it's been a great job. But now I'm passing the power to someone else. There was a runner-up in the Mystery Person contest. Another fantastic writer came in right behind me. And that person is now, officially, the new Mystery Person."

Henry bit deep into his sandwich. Until this moment, he had never liked herring sandwiches.

Maggie continued, "Thank you for reading me, and

I hope you will like tomorrow's column. And now I'm signing off for the last time, Mysteriously Yours, Maggie Marmelstein."

Everyone got up and crowded around Maggie. Ellen hugged her. "Oh, Maggie, thank you for my column. I should have guessed you wrote it."

"You almost did," said Maggie. Then she said, "I think I should tell you about tomorrow's column." And Maggie spoke very softly into Ellen's ear. Ellen giggled. "You're daring, Maggie."

Maggie beamed. Today kids were admiring her as the Mystery Person. Tomorrow they would admire her as a brave newspaper person.

Henry continued to eat his sandwich. He was now the Mystery Person, somebody with a secret identity. Noah whispered to him, "Congratulations and one bit of advice, Henry. Watch out for fainters."

Tamara walked away. Ronald ran after her, still waving the paper, and shouting, "Don't give up, Tamara. Don't give up! This is worth at least half a jelly bean!"

Maggie was so excited she forgot to finish her Swiss cheese sandwich and two saltines.

27
"Dear Loyal Readers . . ."

• •
****

It was early Tuesday morning. Noah walked into Miss Stemmish's room. Piles of newspapers were on her desk.

"Good morning, Noah," she said. "Ready to deliver the newspapers?"

"Ready," said Noah. "How did the Mystery Person column come out?"

"Exactly as you phoned it in on Friday afternoon," said Miss Stemmish.

"Yes, I see," said Noah as he read the column.

Dear Loyal Readers of the
Mystery Person column,
  We have received our first
letter to the editor about the
Mystery Person column. The
Mystery Person and I, Noah
Moore your editor, agree that
all opinions have merit,
although some have less merit
than others. So in the
tradition of fine, impartial,
and rather brave journalism
we are sharing our first

letter with you. Dissenting
opinions will be most welcome.

Dear Mystery Person,
Your column is the pits.
Yours Truly,
Ronald the Rock Thrower

Noah whistled as he delivered the newspapers.

Mystery Muffins

The first thing to remember when you're making Mystery Muffins is that some muffins are more mysterious than others. My top mystery ingredients are cloves, cinnamon, walnuts, and apples. But walnuts and apples are easy to identify, mostly by their crunch, so you might want to use mystery ingredients that can easily hide out in the muffin mix.

Ingredients

- 2 cups flour
- $\frac{1}{3}$ cup sugar
- $\frac{1}{2}$ teaspoon salt
- 3 teaspoons baking powder
- 2 eggs (beaten)
- 2 tablespoons melted butter or margarine (but if you don't know how to melt, use 2 tablespoons vegetable oil)
- $\frac{3}{4}$ cup milk
- a small sprinkle of ground cloves (m. i.)*
- a very big sprinkle of cinnamon (m. i.)*
- $\frac{1}{2}$ cup chopped or torn-apart walnuts (m. i.)*
- pieces of an apple (m. i.)*

Greased muffin tins: enough to hold about twelve big muffins.

---

* mystery ingredient

Instructions

Sift together all the nonmysterious dry ingredients into a bowl. Then mix in everything else, mysterious and nonmysterious. Mix just long enough so there aren't any dry spots showing. After you do it, the mix will probably look ugly, but don't pay any attention to that.

Next, fill greased muffin tins two-thirds full with the mix. Now here's where you pay a lot of attention, because you'll be baking with a very hot oven. Besides attention, you need big mitts. Bake everything in a 400° oven for about twenty minutes.

You should land up with about twelve big muffins. Sometimes the muffins look ugly, which you should have been prepared for when you saw how ugly the mix looked. But sometimes the muffins look beautiful, which is a nice surprise, except they get eaten up faster.

Wonderfully Vile
Liver Crackers

Ingredients

a hunk (about $\frac{1}{2}$ cup) of raw liver, cut up (more
about this later)
  2 tablespoons very chopped onion
  1 clove garlic, minced and mashed
  $\frac{1}{2}$ teaspoon salt
$1\frac{1}{2}$ cups sifted flour
  $\frac{1}{3}$ cup oil
  1 teaspoon caraway seeds
additional flour to flour pastry board
additional sprinkle salt or garlic salt

Instructions

Notice that I have used words like "cut up,"
"chopped," "minced," and "mashed." Disintegration
is the key to this recipe. Make sure the liver is cut
or mashed into such small pieces that it's liquidy.

Mix garlic, onion, and salt (but not the additional salt)
together, and then add your liquidy liver and mix all
together. Add oil. Mix again. Add flour (but not the
additional flour) very slowly. (Dump some, mix some,
dump some, mix some, et cetera.)

Sprinkle caraway seeds over the mixture and stir them in well. Then press the mess into a round shape very tightly with your hands. (This is the vilest part, so pretend it's not liver.)

Put the mixture on the pastry board, which should already be floured with your additional flour, and roll it flat with a rolling pin. Then try to roll the mixture onto the rolling pin and transport it onto a large baking sheet. If that doesn't work, transport the mixture to the baking sheet any way you can.

Now flatten it once again with the rolling pin to about $\frac{1}{8}$ inch thickness. When you're all flattened out, cut it into about two dozen squares. Sprinkle with the additional sprinkle of salt and bake at 350° (remember your mitts) for thirty minutes. If you did everything right, after about fifteen minutes of baking, your kitchen should smell like burning rubber. When the thirty minutes are up, remove the sheet of crackers from the oven. Cool before eating. Better still, don't eat them at all.

Acknowledgments for Wonderfully Vile Liver Crackers

Many thanks:

to that eminent Baker, Betty, for her cracker recipe,

to Mitchell Sharmat, for vilely adapting the recipe and baking twenty-four crackers,

but most of all, gratefully, to my dog Fritz Melvin Sharmat, for eating them up.